I carry a brick on my shoulder in order that
the world may know what my house was like.

—BERTOLT BRECHT

A PAGAN PLACE

Dan Egan is in Drewsboro
The Wattles at the gate
Manny Parker's in the Avenue
And the Nigger's walking straight.

Manny Parker was a botanist, out in all weathers, lived with his sister that ran the sweetshop, they ate meat Fridays, they were Protestants. Your mother dealt there, found them honest.

They put chocolate aside for her because it was rationed, six bars of plain and six bars of fruit and nut. These she stored in the sideboard along with jams and jellies. The sideboard was dark brown, the keys missing, but since the doors opened with a terrible creak it was nearly the same as having them locked. No one opened those doors without the whole house knowing. When the bitter oranges came from Seville in the spring, Manny Parker's sister made a marmalade and the pound pots were put to cool on the counter where everyone could see them and compliment her on them. She favored a coarser marmalade than your mother and the shreds suspended in the dark jelly were like seeing pet fish in a tank.

The Wattles were in the gate lodge, across the road from

the gates. The gates were green, and speared along the top, the hasp missing. One gate was loose in its pivot and when it slipped out you had to hold on for dear life or you fell, gate and all.

They were named the Wattles because their daughter Lizzie went to Australia and came home, and had yellow jaundice. Before she came she sent snaps of herself and they got the Gramophone mended and bought a record Far Away in Australia but she said that was the last thing she wanted to hear and asked bitterly where the pipers were. She threatened to go back but didn't. The Wattles never opened gates because they didn't get paid. The two old people had the pension.

Mr. Wattle called everyone Mister and when Mrs. Wattle bought a cane chair he said Am I in my own house at all Mister? When the cow did number two into the pail of milk, Mr. Wattle who was milking didn't see it. The women strained the milk over and over again through a strainer and through muslin but it was still yellow and it smelled. The other time when milk had a smell was when the cows were given turnips or the grass was too rich.

That rich grass was called aftergrass and your father prized it for his horses. If the gates were left open, or if the big stone was not put to them, cattle got in or got out and either ways there were ructions, investigations as to who was to blame. Your mother could not bear to see and hear stray cattle dispersing all over the fields because she had a presentiment that they were going to be there forever, fattening themselves for free. Yet they were never turned out. Only the tinker's stock was driven out. Tinkers' ponies were canny. They grazed on the roadside, never shied when cars and lorries went by and if they saw a guard coming had the good sense to saunter off. The tinkers settled in the evicted field that belonged to no one because two married brothers fought over it and neither would let the other till it. Some nights there were lots of caravans there with lights shining through the half doors, some nights it was like every other field, dark and empty and dangerous.

Dan Egan was dead but his name lived on because there was a tree named after him, a horse chestnut. Boys shook it for conkers and if they got caught they got a hammering from your father. Dan Egan was buried over on the island where your mother said she would not go because there would be no passers-by to pray for the repose of her soul. You were afraid your mother might die, before you.

Over on the island there were birds and ruins. The ruins had metal plaques on them saying what period in history they were built in. Saints and scholars had lived there. One door had a lintel with four recesses and the stones were as brittle as bread crumbs. Visitors went in rowboats and walked around the ruins. On a fine day the surface of the lake glittered like tin but it never happened to be like that for a regatta.

There were cattle on the island belonging to the butcher, bullocks. They made themselves at home on the graves, disentangled the wreaths, trampled on the glass domes and chewed flowers that were supposed to be everlasting. Those flowers were of calcium and looked like bones but no corpses showed above the ground because the graves were dug deep.

If dead people appeared it could only be at night, the way Dan Egan was said to appear under the shade of the tree named after him. Whenever his name was mentioned your father said Poor devil, God rest him. Your father and he got drunk together, played cards and clicked girls. Your father didn't mention girls but there was a photo of them both on a sidecar, each with a girl, and each couple with a rug over the knees. It was taken at the Horse Show to which they went annually. They went everywhere together although Dan Egan was a lot older. When the lake was frozen they walked nine miles to an all-night dance, and Dan Egan insisted on dragging a boat behind them and your father was bucking, but providential it was because on the way home in the morning the ice began to go. When they got in the boat they found they had no oars and Dan Egan was cursing and blinding and they were bobbing around like that between the floats of ice until a coal boat went by at midday.

Your father met your mother at that dance but didn't throw two words to her. Your mother was all dolled up, home from America on holiday, had a long dress and peroxide in her hair. Your mother put the eye on him then and got her brother to invite him up to their house to walk the land.

Your father could guess the acreage of any field by walking it. That and horses was his hobby and off nights with Dan Egan for sing-songs and out on the lake shooting duck. Dan Egan and he lived in a big house with an old tiddly nanny and when they got home drunk in the mornings she used to bring up shaving water and whisky, a mug of each. Kept a roaring fire they did in one room and in all the other rooms there were bats, and mice, and dark pieces of furniture.

Your father was an orphan but his old tiddly nanny took care of him and when he wanted shaving water or a headache powder all he had to do was press a bell and when the green gong trembled in the kitchen his old tiddly nanny said Bad cess to you but went to him all the same.

Your father burned the house sooner than let the Black and Tans occupy it as a barracks. Not even a candlestick or a cruet could he take away as a memento because that would have been theft. The house got burned but the old cellar remained and your mother used it as a dumping ground. Your mother dumped ashes there and the empties that were not charged on and broken crockery and the entrails of the cockerels that got killed and drawn every Saturday in summer, in preparation for Sunday's dinner. She gave herself the worst parts of the chicken, the skin, the Pope's nose, the posterior bits. She sent one once a month to your sister Emma along with a cake and some butter.

Emma had airs because she was born in New York. Often she slighted you and said you were trash and said Be off, trash. She pedaled fiercely on her bicycle so that you couldn't catch up.

She was his favorite. He called her Whitehead. She got the watch. The watch made a black rim on her wrist and she told you that was known as oxidization. She had a bracelet too that was expandable. Once it got caught above her elbow and had to be damped and forced down. It got buckled.

There was not much jewelry lying about the house, his gold watch, some necklaces, and loose pearls in a soapdish that were skinless and without glow. Your house had no gongs either, and no cellar, but it had marble mantelpieces in all the rooms and constellations of flowers in the centers of the ceilings.

In the chimneys crows nested. Crows preferred the chimneys to the trees because the trees were prey to the wind.

Around the tree trunks were plaits of ivy so thick and matted that they were like shields. The crows pecked at the ivy. They were black and lustrous and were always on the go, circling around and around, cawing and crying.

What was classified as a front garden had pampas grass, Devil's pokers, and apple trees that hadn't grown to their full stature but weren't dwarfs either. The pampas grass was in wayward clusters, more blue than green. It was a foreign grass, stiff in stem and with a knife edge. It was from the old days, the gone days, when the place had its ornamental garden. You put that part of your hand between thumb and forefinger to the knife edge, that flap which if it got cut could lead to lockjaw. That was courting disaster. The grass was scythed once a month, the hedge clipped. Nettles had to be kept at bay. Nettles had a white flower that no one admired. She sent you around the fields to gather some for young chickens. She gave you a saucepan and shears and told you to drop them directly as you cut them, so as to protect your hands. You suffered a few stings to be devout. You crooned and baritoned in order to intimidate small animals that were lurking in briars and low coverts of foliage. Nettles had an iron content. Cabbage had iodine. Cabbage was frequently on the menu. It was one of her specialities. She was liberal with salt and pepper and these condiments combined with cabbage and mashed potatoes made a lovely compound. Good with turnips too or for that matter any of the root vegetables. If there was fresh meat he had it, a chop nicely done. The dogs got the bone. They tussled over it. They were huge and were the color of lions. They were called Bran and Shep, Bran after an ancient hero's dog and Shep because it was such a convenient name. They went off at night, across fields, so did badgers and hares and foxes and wildcats and owls and rats and weasels and moles, all enemies, all springing at each other, all letting out their primeval cries. In the morning on the way to school, you saw things, tracks, fur, feathers, and once a paw with its long nails intact. You skirted the fort of dark trees.

It was a pagan place and circular. Druids had their rites there long before your mother and father or his mother and father or her mother and father or anyone you'd ever heard tell of. But Mr. Wattle said that was not all, said he had seen a lady ungirdled there one night on his way home from physicking the donkey. The ground inside was shifty, a swamp where lilies bloomed. They were called bog lilies. The donkey went in there to die and no wonder because the shelter was ample. No one would go in to bury it. It decomposed. The smell grew worse and worse and more and more rampant. The dogs carried the members around, the bits, big bones and little bones, and they were scattered everywhere and in the end were as brown and as odorless as twigs.

The dogs had a routine. They slept during the day. They had places under the hedge hollowed out to their shape and they moved around the house depending on the elements. The wind ruffled their coats, drew attention to the ranges of tawny in them. They were half brothers, had had the same mother, a Shep, but conflicting fathers. They convoyed her when she went to Manny Parker's sister's shop to collect chocolate or to pay something off her bill. Her bill was unending. No sooner had she paid something than she made a new purchase but there was an understanding between her and Manny Parker's sister, a tacit understanding.

You always ran home from school. Your friends jeered.

Called you sutach, called you suck-suck, called you diddums and spoilsport and clown and pissabed. On the way home from Mass diarrhea ran all down your legs and you got behind the wall and stayed there until everyone had gone, the men tearing to the pub, the doctor and Hilda in their cars, the people on bicycles, the pedestrians and the sacristan who had had to stay behind to quench candles and lock the big oak door. Your mother was not vexed, said it could happen to a bishop. Your friends passed remarks about it, wrote notes to each other, referred to it as the Incident. Your friend Jewel wrote on the blackboard to remember the Incident, marmalade in color, behind a certain wall on the Sabbath day.

Before your first Holy Communion Jewel and you practiced receiving the Host. You received bits of paper from each other. You had to hold it for as long as possible, for as long as it was likely to take the body and blood of Jesus to melt into you. The bits of paper soaked up all your saliva but it was not a sin when they grazed your teeth whereas it would be a sin if the Host were to. That was your main preoccupation on your first Holy Communion day, even though you were being admired by all and sundry because of your finery. Your shoes were buckskin and your veil had sprays of lily of the valley wrought into it. Yours was the finest veil. Your mother saw to that. Our Lord didn't touch your teeth but there was a crisis afterwards. When Lizzie asked you to pose for a snap you stood against the railing and a corner of the veil blew up and got caught on a spear and would have been in shreds only that the priest rescued it. Your mother went on about what a close shave it was and you got five shillings and there were sun showers and that was your first Holy Communion. Jewel had a tea party to which you were not invited. Your friends were not friends the way your father and Dan Egan were.

When your father talked of Dan Egan his eyes filled up with tears. He and Dan Egan were arrested as they walked out of a public house and unfortunate it was because Dan Egan was carrying a bulldog revolver. Told the Black and Tans it was for shooting hares and rabbits but the Tans didn't swallow that, and the pair of them were shoved in the lorry and brought to the nearest jail.

Tied together they were and inveigled to split on their comrades but they didn't and they even got kicked and belted but they didn't give in. Bound together all night without being let talk and had their faces dipped in a rain barrel whenever either one of them nodded off. Grigged too, with stories of what they would fancy for supper, trout or chicken. And when Dan Egan had to do number two they were still tied together and that made them buddies forever.

They were let out in the morning with a warning, but when they got out on the street no one would give them a lift home and they had to walk without benefit of either tea or whisky. From the beltings he got, Dan Egan developed epileptic fits and when the Free State was established he applied for a pension and was given it, but your father got none and they came to blows and a coolness set in.

Once he died, they became the best of friends again and your father often told of the evening soon after their arrest when they set fire to the big house and how methodical they were—soaked doors and wainscoting and floors and window frames all with petrol, and drenched rags which they scattered around. Your father told how they had to wait for nightfall and how all that long day they told stories and split matches and how just before they did it Dan Egan said he'd give his eyesight to see the Tans' faces when they saw a conflagration on the site that was to have been their headquarters. The Tans had it all worked out that they'd occupy your father's house being as it was spacious with ample accommodation for themselves and for prisoners, with fireplaces, and woods nearby, an indoor pump, a ballroom, everything a battalion would need. When they'd done the deed they had to run for it, and in opposite directions along back roads and byroads. When your father got to the house that was supposed to shelter him they had the wind up so he had to go on and on, shanks-maring it, and finally the people who took him in were strangers altogether but they treated him nicely.

He hid in a potato pit. It was there he contracted eczema and it stayed with him all his life and he had to get yellow ointment for it, from a woman who did cures. She cured warts and fits and your mother said she would not like to get in her black books because she wouldn't be surprised if she was a witch. There was always smoke from her chimney and around her window, wraiths of it. At Mass she reeked of smoke and no one wanted to sit near her. She picked plants and gathered stones and when foraging she cackled to herself. She was a widow.

When your father crawled out of the potato pit at night his legs were weak as water and when he went across to the farmhouse there were girls there singing and cutting up seed potatoes for sowing. It must have been spring. Your father never asked them their names. Your father said how in the old days people would give you a shilling or take you in but your mother said that was all baloney and that distance lends enchantment and he told her she didn't know what she was talking about because she didn't know Dan Egan or any of these people and she said no she didn't, but very standoffish like she didn't want to.

Jobbers she called them, his friends—the cattle dealers, the horse dealers, the feather merchants, and Sacco.

Sacco came; he did tricks with matches and with a handkerchief, then he moved the lamp to appoint the shadow and with thumb and forefinger he did a movement that was like rabbits' paws dancing on a wall. He made four shadows with only two fingers, one set higher than the other. That was magic. He was a magician. He had steel-rimmed spectacles. He complimented her on her bread. Before she cut it there was a perfect sign of the cross on the top where she had etched it unthinkingly on the raw dough. Sacco began to describe the marriage pattern. He said it was love at first, frequent journeys to the bed, matinee and evening performance, the hay not saved, the calves not fed, then after the first child a bit of a cooling off, the man going out nights and the subsequent children begotten in drink, then squabbles, ructions, first Holy Communions, shoes having to be bought, a lot of troubles and late in life the man back at his own fireplace spitting and banging and grunting inanities to his own wife.

Your mother was furious, nearly took the cake of bread away. Your father changed the conversation, asked when the fair at Spancehill was. Sacco not only knew the day but had advance information on the breeds of ponies that were going to be on sale there.

You knew your father and the Nigger would go together,

the Nigger would put on his leggings and his accoutrements and your father would choose one of his soft felt hats, and bid for ponies he had no need of. They would lead them home—gray ponies or dappled—on a master reins and intern them in a house for a few days until they forgot the presence of their own mares and the sniff of their own lands. They would break them in then.

Your father had given the Nigger a site and that meant he had a right of way and he went in and out at all hours, tearing drunk. They christened him the Nigger because he had berries on one cheek that were the color of beetroot and when he moved his jaw they swayed and made everybody laugh. Some called them carbuncles. On fair days and race days strangers bought pints for him, to do the trick with the jaw. Though they laughed and split themselves laughing, he himself never did, he just did the trick and downed the pints.

Going home drunk he took off his breeches by the water pump and when girls and women went by, he said Come here missie, until I do pooly in you, but if the guards or the sergeant went by he insisted that he was having a footbath. The girls used to fly past and when he couldn't catch them he did pooly anyhow, that was not pooly at all but white stuff. Then he went on home cursing and blinding and laughing like a jackass.

Your mother said he would burn the house, which was a shack, over his head, and that he would die without a priest. He kept a roaring fire going and he read all the old almanacs and knew the predictions about wars and weather and the end of the world and things. His hero was Christopher Columbus. He used the almanacs as handles to grip the kettle and though the edges were scorched he never let the words burn, he loved the words.

Your father said he made a great cup of tea, your mother said it was like senna. Your mother tackled him one day, asked when he was moving on to his own part of the country and his relatives.

He looked at her, he said You're an ignorant woman, I hasten to tell you, you're an ignorant woman. After that he went in and out with a sack over his head so that she couldn't accost him.

Your father said what harm was it to give right of way and a bit of land to a poor man that needed it. Poor man, she said, sourly.

Your mother and father were goodnatured in two different ways. Your mother sent slab cake and eggs to Della, the girl who had consumption, but your father gave potatoes away and turf banks and pasture. Often there was strife over it.

One day your father had a pitchfork raised to your mother and said I'll split the head of you open and your mother said And when you've done it there will be a place for you. And you were sure that he would and you and your sister Emma were onlookers and your sister Emma kept putting twists of paper in her hair, both to curl it and to pass the time. Later when your mother felt your pulse she said it was not normal, nobody's pulse was normal that particular day.

Later still, when your mother told her sister, your Aunt Bride, she added things that did not happen, like that the prongs of the fork were on her temples and heading for her eyes, like that she stamped her foot and dared him to. Which she didn't. She added touches of bravery. An emergency might have occurred but that Ambie came to the rescue.

Ambie lived in your house but was always threatening to go. He and the Nigger were mortal enemies, Ambie stood up for your mother and the Nigger sided with your father. They could not be left alone, together, for fear of attacking each other over political issues. They had to be together when the cattle were being hauled into the lorry and sent to the city to a mart.

The city butchers favored the cattle that came from the sweet land. The grass differed from place to place, was sweet, was sour, was saline, depending on the mineral content. The clover made it sweetest of all and the cows even munched the clover flower.

It took three men to get them into the lorry. They were up at cockcrow. It was teeming. The beasts kept slipping and sliding over the runway and Ambie and the Nigger were cursing and blinding at each other and the beasts were bawling, and no one could get heard. Ambie positioned himself on the back of the lorry, intending to grab them by the horns as they were hustled up, but it was a right tug-of-war between him and them, they trying to pull him down and he trying to pull them up and the Nigger saying Shag whenever Ambie let go and the beasts slipped back down again. It took the best part of an hour. Afterwards everything was very quiet and the dogs were disappointed when all the commotion died down.

Your mother said that their language was choice but she was not scandalized as she was hoping that the cattle would fetch a good price.

She told Ambie that they would never have got dispatched but for his presence of mind. From time to time she flattered him. She was afraid he might take a figari and leave.

He was saving money. He earned extra money through the killing of pigs, at which he was adept. He had his own knife and his own spattered overalls. He slit their throats then held them upside down over a container to catch the blood that was essential for the black puddings. You seldom watched but you heard. The squeals of each particular pig reached you no matter where you hid, no matter where you happened to crouch, and it was heart-rending as if the pig was making a last but futile appeal to someone to save him. Hens never did that, hens only wriggled and expired.

The dogs did not like those squeals either, they hid under the table and appeared only when there was offal and things being sorted out, not that they ate it, they merely examined it. They had selective tastes.

Your mother gave strips of pork away, the choice bits to the professional people, the doctor, Manny Parker's sister, and the sergeant; the cottagers got lesser pieces, knuckles, and crubeens for boiling. It took hours allocating the different portions. When you delivered them you got praise or sometimes a sixpence.

At card games Ambie cheated and won geese and turkeys which he sold. Before he sold them he stuffed them with oats to put the weight up. Some buyers were crafty and waited for the geese and turkeys to do number two and the tailor's wife presided with the brass scales.

Ambie shot a neighbor's goose and would have got summonsed only your father squared it with the guards. Your father had influence, got a crime hushed up a long time before, not for himself, but for one of his friends. One of his friends shot a girl because she wouldn't serve him another drink, shot and missed. But it was still a crime and the man was charged with attempted manslaughter. And your father went and saw the girl and her mother and gave them soft soap and money. The man was deported to Australia instead of getting jailed and he was never heard of again and your mother said that was destiny for you.

Your father was a peace commissioner and spoke up for Ambie, said the shooting of the goose was accidental, said Ambie thought it was a wild swan that had strayed in off the lake. Normally they were at loggerheads, disagreed about everything, how to foot turf, or how to treat a dog for distemper.

Ambie came from a rocky place where hardly anything grew and where the small fields were divided by stone walls instead of grass banks or lines of trees. At Easter time they killed a kid there. That was their speciality. His mother sent your mother a red Christmas candle. His mother and your mother had never met. Ambie carried the candle the whole way, in his left hand, and only when he was getting down off the bicycle did it snap and your mother said A bull in a china shop and Ambie laughed as he handed it to her.

When she got cross you quaked but Ambie had a different ploy, he sucked air between his teeth. His teeth were rotten. He sucked air or he twiddled the signet ring that was made of aluminum. It was aluminum culled from a plane that had crashed. People went to look at the wreckage the way they went to look at scenery or quins if they had been born. It was a two-seater German plane that crashed by mistake. The pilot went into the sea. There were notes about it between heads of government. But it did not break hearts the way the doctor's death did, because the pilot was a stranger. There were bits of him everywhere and parts of the car were taken as souvenirs. Your father took a door handle.

The doctor crashed into a telegraph pole and everyone said he must have had home brew taken. The telegraph pole was new, otherwise he would have known it, because he knew that road backwards. A hurley field got christened after him. He had had two wives but he never acknowledged the second one and when patients asked how she was he always said My wife is deceased. His second wife was drunk at first Mass, fell off the end of the seat into the aisle. When he got killed she went away and was never heard tell of again. Then the new doctor came and he and his wife were all the rage at first, and had card games specially in their honor. His wife had a teddy-bear coat and a flapjack and said that her people were people of note. Your mother said she was artificial. They kept their bread in an enamel tin with Soiled Dressings written on it.

When your mother tore her vein on the rim of the milk bucket Ambie went for the doctor on the bicycle. She was in the house by the time he came. There were dark gunnels of blood in the rifts between the flagstones so that he could see what he was walking into. The hens were mesmerized by it and pecked at it if you can call that pecking.

He knew where to tie the vein and wrapped clean white gauze around and around it. He refused the ten-shilling note that was offered as a fee. It was a crinkled note retrieved from under the oilcloth of the kitchen table. There was a small set-to. Your father insisted that the doctor take it, stuffed it in his pocket behind his spotted silk handkerchief. The doctor rolled it up like a toffee paper and flung it far away. It flew over the top of the oil lamp and landed in the corner of the window ledge near a spool of black thread. It was a lovely moment, the lids of the stove gleaming, your mother speechless and grateful like a heroine in a play, the doctor accepting a cup of buttermilk, and your father remonstrating but in gratitude. The hairpin on the globe of the lamp gave out a little clatter as the lamp warmed up. Your father sang,

Oh doctor, dear doctor
Oh dear Doctor John
Your codliver oil is so pure and so strong,
I'm afraid of my life
I'll go down in your sight
If I drink any more of your codliver oil.

Sang in admiration even though it was a song composed for the other doctor, the dead doctor who'd crashed.

Your mother did not want to hear an account of his death again. It turned her stomach. The other thing that turned her stomach was breast-feeding and shellfish. You heard her telling Mrs. Durack so, when Mrs. Durack was having a baby and though your mother stressed the direness of her nausea, Mrs. Durack kept saying, You don't say.

Mrs. Durack had her hair veined in the center and then drawn back into a bun and people said she did it to look like Mrs. Simpson who was in love with the Prince of Wales. At their wedding Mrs. Durack sang There's a Bridle Hanging on the Wall and sang very screechy and all the locals thought she was going to be a toff but soon she lost her airs and had improvements made in her husband's pub and a sink put in.

There were thirty pubs in the village. They did business at night. In the daytime they were cold and had to be scrubbed out but at night when the blinds were drawn and the men assembled they were enthralling places. Ambie went every night and your father went periodically. If women went they were put in a place partitioned off by frosted glass and your mother used to cross-examine Ambie on the drinks they had had and the condition they went home in.

Ambie often got you a bar of chocolate and presented it to you in the morning. It was usually dark chocolate with white cream in it. The shopkeepers had their cronies and could decide who to give rationed things to. Once Ambie got you a Peggy's leg that was cinnamon colored and sticky. Your mother didn't mind if you ate it before breakfast, your mother spoiled you, let you make little loaves which she affixed to the top of the big loaf before consigning it to the hot oven, let you put on her dance dresses which were nearly in shreds. During Lent and Advent you didn't eat the chocolate, saved it up, and it was like owning a shop having so many bars all at once, and an assortment.

Ambie went from one pub to the next, depending on where the activity was. Your mother did her best to keep your father in at night, kept up a roaring fire, praised the programs on the wireless, rubbed his head. The smell of his scalp got under her nails, that and the scurf. If in spite he turned the wick too high, the mantle got black and fell away in a shroud of soot. She kept an eye to it, turned it down when he went out to relieve himself. Did it from the top step and always aimed at the same place of flag, night after night. The flag had many a feature, rims of rust where buckets and rain barrels had lain, a lodge of slime around the metal lid that concealed the manhole, repeated hen-droppings and chicken-droppings, which were not the same thing, and a bleached bit where the rain fell perpendicularly without either wall or hedge to deflect its course.

No three days went by without rain occurring on two of them. That was due to being in the Gulf Stream. You learned so in geography. You learned geography by heart and important dates in history and human touches of history as well, such as that Brian Boru got stabbed on the strand at Clontarf, got stabbed by a wicked Dane while giving thanks to God. You knew where straw hats were manufactured, and sewing machines, and cutlery. Your teacher Miss Davitt said how Shane O'Neill was disarmingly attractive and that Queen Elizabeth was light about him which was why she tried to have him poisoned at a feast because Hell has no music like a woman playing second fiddle.

Miss Davitt had no romance at all. She had a cataract in one eye. A cataract was a little cloud that came down over the eye like a veil. There was another kind of cataract that meant running water. Everything meant more than one thing. Miss Davitt was too brainy. She got excited when she discussed politics. Your father and her had a flaming row one night and you were afraid to go to school next day in case she avenged it on you, which she did. She called you a snib, kept referring to the day when she sent you down for twopenceworth of chalk and you misheard and came back with twopenceworth of a chop.

She was for de Valera and your father was for Cosgrave. Cosgrave's crowd sent blueshirts to fight for General Franco in Spain. Your father's seer was an ex-minister for agriculture, who when a heckler threw the question How many toes has a pig? said Take off your boots and count. Your father relished that story and told it when he was in good form and sang Sweet Slievenaman, the song to the mountain that enshrined woman. He sang one way when he was drunk and another when he was sober.

When you were born he and his brother were at issue, but

upon hearing the good news they burst into song, sang Red River Valley through the nose and fell over the bed trying to get a gawk at you, to discern your sex, and your features. The midwife said you were lovely but said it out of shock so preposterous were you. They sang in first and seconds and your father used the unfinished roll of lint to conduct with. The midwife stitched your mother, made a botch of it. Your mother didn't tell you these things but you knew them. You were there then and comprehending.

After she'd done her day's work you sat on her lap. You put your ear to the wall of her stomach and you could hear her insides glugging away, what you felt through one ear was transmitted through the other, her heartbeat, the busyness of her digestion and the leisureliness of her breath. Your father told you to get down out of there, to get down. Put his hand under her chin and forced her face up, told her to smile, smile, told her she was getting old, told her she had wrinkles, called her Mud, short for mother. She had to go across the landing to his room. An edict.

The landing was big and cold. There was a sofa that never got sat on and a fringed mat that hardly ever got shook out. There was an embroidered picture that said There's a rose in the heart of New York. A funny thing to say. You saw New York on a postcard and it was all skyscrapers.

Before she went across the landing she put tissue paper in the inside of her pussy. It made a crinkly noise. Even without a candle you knew what she was doing. She saved tissue paper from the boxes that new shoes came in. Over there she moaned and groaned. His sinews crackled. You ate sweets, small chocolate buttons that congealed on the roof of the mouth.

You were frightened of lockjaw and also of being kidnapped. In your mother you were safe and that was the only time you couldn't get kidnapped and that was the nearest you ever were to any other human being. Between you and your mother there was only a membrane, wafer thin. Being near someone on the inside was not the same thing as being near them on the outside, even though the latter could involve hugging and kissing.

Once you were one with her. She didn't like it. She told the woman with the hair like Mrs. Simpson how she was sick and bilious all the time. You were conceived in New York, where the rose was purported to be.

Emma was born there, long before you, Emma was born soon after they got married. Emma was a love child. Emma learned to walk in a park in New York and was brought to Coney Island and given ice cream.

They had gone there to make their fortune. Your father tried to kill your mother but she said her brother who was a teetotaler would avenge her death and your father said he never could because he was as dead as doornails. And that was the first your mother knew about her brother being dead.

He didn't die a hero's death like he should, being as he was a wanted man and had organized ambushes against the Tans; he died from a bomb that he was using to catch fish with, in the Blackwater River. It exploded. His cartridge belt got soldered to his stomach and when the ambulance came all they could do was gather the bits into a blanket. Just before he died he spoke a letter to his mother and a priest copied it down, all about God and patriotism and how happy he was to be dying. That letter was in an arbutus frame and when you wanted a good cry you went into the room and read it and the tears came almost as soon as you started to read the words.

You cried at plays too, everyone cried at plays, even the men standing at the back of the hall who minutes before would be talking or laughing. The actors had to shout because of all the sobbing and crying. Handkerchiefs were passed around from one to another, from those who had them to those who had not, among the women that is. The men used the cuff of their coats and blew snot between their fingers and threw it from them like butts of apple.

She never kissed you goodnight, there was no need for that. When you turned to the wall she turned too, put her arms around you, underneath your ribs, clenched you once or twice. You prayed, she prayed, the same prayer.

As I lay me down to sleep
I pray to God my soul to keep
And if I die before I wake
I pray to God my soul to take.

You did not want her to die.

Her own mother nearly took her own life once, went out to the hayshed with the carving knife, having bade goodbye to everyone like it was a proper bed scene. Her own father was a toper too. History repeating itself. The crucifix sometimes slipped out of her hand and fell in the warm bed between you. The metal edges wakened you up.

She often dreamed that she was back in New York and was grieved to find herself in the blue room with the uncultivated hills and the boring fields around her. The hills were old mountains, mountains that had lost their peaks and that is why she often said she felt as old as the hills. They were always either misted over or were a nice shade of blue. A navy blue like night although it occurred in the morning. The cows came round the paling wire, lowing and lowing.

It was Ambie's job to call her but he overoiled the clock. The tick was like a sputter, the alarm soft and unobtrusive. Your father was bucking. The milk was late for the creamery, three days in a row. The creamery refused it. It had to be thrown out and not even the beasts came to lick it up. It stayed there, in curds on the grass until the rain washed it.

The tankard was green and smelly inside, had to be scalded with several kettles of boiling water whereas normally one kettle full was enough. There was a way of doing it, letting trickles of water down the side of the tank and then rubbing it with a cloth and then swishing the water round the bottom of the tank. When you stuck your head in there was a dank smell and your echo was funny. The strainer had muslin laid into it because the metal holes were too big and straw or anything could get through.

Your father wrote a letter to the creamery manager, a snorter. You were sent with it. The creamery manager was a sissy and his wife was a sissy and they called each other Betty love and Jack darling and he said Are you all right Betty love? and she said If you're all right Jack darling, I'm all right. They shared a prayer book at Mass, took turns with it, it was a missal really, his, from the time he was going to be a priest. It had lots of different colored ribbons to mark the different gospels for the different Sundays and holy days. They had no babies but they had a pram in case they should have babies and the pram was in the porch with logs laid into it. They kept you waiting in the porch. There was a smell of fried onions. The creamery manager came back with you to apologize to your father and your father wasn't abusive at all and told your mother to put the kettle on. Your mother said under her breath that if there was one thing she hated it was two-facedness.

Your mother was very straightforward and committed a terrible sin once, went to a Protestant service, to Manny Parker's mother's funeral, and after perjury that was the biggest sin of all and the priest had to refer it to the bishop. But even after the forgiveness came the priest made a show of her by giving a sermon about it and although he didn't mention her by name everyone knew and she got up in the middle of the sermon and walked out, tapping her umbrella on the tiles as she went. Ambie said she had great gumption to do it.

People said different things depending on who they were talking to. That priest was not a friend of hers but the other priest was and he got sent away because of the greyhounds he kept. He was always occupied with them, walking them, training them, taking them to the tracks on Saturday nights. Put a big gray scarf over his white collar so that he wouldn't be identified as a priest. Gave them codliver oil and had girls' names for most of them. The man that helped him was called Ryan and he was always saying Ryan, give the dogs some water, Ryan, give the dogs some codliver oil, Ryan, give the dogs some oatmeal biscuits. They used to gnaw the jambs of the door, not because they were hungry, but because they were nervous. At Mass, Ambie and others watched like hawks to see how much wine he drank from the chalice, had their doubts about him, used to throw their heads back, imitating his gulps, quaffing, though of course they had nothing to drink only the air. It made them thirsty. After Mass they all converged on the pub to slake their thirst. They went to a pub belonging to the woman who passed biscuits around. She said it was to soak up the porter but your mother said it was to keep men away from their Sunday dinners.

No one ever knew who split to the bishop but it happened that he called on the priest unexpectedly whereas it was a ritual that he came only every three years, for the Confirmation. When he saw the hounds he asked whose they were and the priest couldn't lie, because the bishop would have known it later being as the bishop was the priest's confessor. The priest got transferred, miles away, to a poor parish where there wasn't even a dancehall. Your mother always inquired after him and when she heard that he took to the drink in a big way, she said that at least greyhounds were harmless and that was unusual because she was opposed to all forms of gambling.

She was against your father having horses, even his trophies irritated her. The ribbons that his horses won at shows maddened her and when he had the silver cup for a year she never cleaned it although she was fanatic about preserving silver. She even put vaseline on the cutlery to stop it tarnishing. She used vaseline for piles too and for chapped lips and when the hem of your new coat hurt your bare legs above the knees and made them red she applied vaseline and rubbed it round and round in nice circular movements. That was called ire. The horse that won the cup was called Shannon Rose.

Nearly everybody loved a rose. There were wild roses and tea roses and roses that smelled like apples and the essence of roses was said to be green. Dog roses grew wild on the roadside in June. Hawthorn grew wild too but it was unlucky to bring in the house. Roses were lovely because they were connected with St. Theresa.

If you made a novena to St. Theresa and were given a rose during the nine days of it, it meant your intention would be granted. You made novenas for all sorts of things but especially for your mother and father that they would be happy and that they would get out of debt.

The day the bailiff came he sat you on his knee and asked you what you would like to be when you grew up. You said a domestic economy instructress. You called him Father. He was so nice and kindly that you thought he was a priest. He smiled at that and so did your mother although she was crying just before and shaking holy water and saying Jesus and Mary.

Your father wouldn't come out of the room, he had locked the door and was in there with a revolver. The same room where you sat and put a doll's big soft toe between your legs outside your knickers, and tickled yourself. Your father said he'd shoot if anyone entered. Your mother couldn't figure out where he'd got the cartridges from. The gun was under the table on a spare leaf of wood. You risked splinters if you put your hand in there. Your father had come on the blackberry wine that was fermenting in the various bottles, even though she had put cloths over to disguise them. You could hear a cork popping and then glug glug as he poured. There were glasses in there, cut glasses with stems.

Ambie was missing. Your mother said he never was where he was wanted. She lamented the wine. You and she had picked the blackberries, had gone specially to pick them when the sun shone, because wet blackberries impaired the flavor. You had to examine the base of each one for maggots. Some were overripe and some not ripe at all. Those that were underneath took longer to ripen. But you had to pick some of those because your mother said they improved the flavor, made it tart. Your mother envisaged the wine for happy occasions, for trifles, and for giving to visitors in secret, in the pantry.

Your father was in there over an hour and you all tiptoed around to the side window and it transpired that he had gone to sleep. The same window where honey bees got in one summer and Ambie thought to catch them, and he sent your mother in with a sheet over her head and when she got stung she let out a scream, and said Oh Jesus, does it have two stings?

Your father was fast asleep, his backside at the very edge of the chair. It could have resulted in his falling off but it didn't. His long legs were stretched ahead of him. Your mother lifted you up to see. There was wine spilled on the lino, the bottle had overturned. She held you so close to the wall that the stones grazed your knees. That was a good thing because you had suffered and God would note that suffering and put it toward easing her predicament.

The bailiff went in to get the revolver and your mother kept begging him to be careful, be careful. It was little and rusted but lethal all the same. He said he had used one like it. He was all thumbs and she had to call to him to point it elsewhere before touching the catch. He had to spin a thing to tip the cartridges out and it was so stiff that he had to do that more than once. She kneeled to retrieve them. When she took the revolver she said it was up in the river it would go. Its fighting days were over.

She and you waited in the field and when you saw a light

being struck in the room you remarked that your father had come awake and was lighting a cigarette. She prayed for the safety of the house. You were afraid of Druids. You had things to fear from the living and from the dead.

Later she had Mass said in that room. She sent for grapefruit for the priest's breakfast but Ambie cut it the wrong way, cut it so it had no center to insert the cherry in. Your mother said he was a yahoo. Her other sarcastic names for him were plebeian and aborigine. The cherries were soaked in a liqueur. There were other cherries that were in a carton and were all glued together and they were glacé. People's eyes were glacé, when they were upset or when they had fever. The priest blessed the house, shook holy water from a thurible all over furniture and things, but didn't bless the people. Only newly ordained priests could do that.

There was a local priest in the South Seas that everyone was in love with. You often invented situations where you were his sacristan, ironing his vestments and things, serving him but hardly ever encountering him. His name was Father Declan.

When the parish priest was finished blessing, Ambie came in for the leavings, and ate them out of his hand. He ate grapefruit pulp, bacon, and a piece of brown bread all together. He sang

Oh Miss Nicholas,
Don't be so ridiculous,
I don't like it in the daytime.
Night time is the right time
Afternoon or evening that's too soon,
So Miss Nicholas,

Don't be so ridiculous,
I don't like it in the noon . . .

Miss Nicholas was the priest's housekeeper, a woman of
fifty, with warts. Your mother closed the door so that Ambie
could not be heard, then opened it and stuck her head
in and made a face, then slammed it again. The priest was
in the hall saying goodbye. There was money being put in
his pocket because he was thanking them in a conciliatory
tone. He knew how badly off they were. Ambie stopped
singing.

You told him that the greatest line ever written was by
Shakespeare. And it was, This is my beloved son in whom I
am well pleased. Ambie said they get their money easy, the
priests and the Shakespeares. Ambie was a prime boy. Ambie
got the doctor's maid into trouble and she put newspapers all
over her bed after she drank ergot and even at that the blood
soaked right down through the mattress and she had to sleep
on springs until it dried out. The doctor's wife locked her in
the room for five days and starved her.

The doctor and your mother sat on the kitchen table next
to one another and her legs were down, and his hand was
somewhere under her apron, in the unknown, tinkering, and
she was not laughing and she was not crying but the sounds
were like laughing and crying rolled into one, and she was
flushed. You took the dog by its mane and ran off. When
you came back she was asking the doctor if he thought her
plates were disgraceful. She had a display of plates on the
dresser, some with fruits on them and others with represen-
tations of Japanese people that had a sad love story attached
to them. The mad woman had told her her plates were dis-

graceful. The doctor said on the contrary that the dresser was as the poem depicted — filled with shining delft, speckled and white and blue and brown. Many were held together with gum. The dried gum made a brown smear along the face of the plate but from a distance and in an evening light they looked perfect.

Your father broke a platter, did it when looking for the strap of a safety razor. He lost his temper and threw the platter. It smashed on the tiled floor. She looked for the strap in the oak press, where fletches of bacon were stored. There were wings there too, white wings and gray wings, the wings of geese and turkeys, their handles a knuckle that oozed grease. The saltpeter was like frosting on the strap of the razor. He swung it like he was intending to hit someone. He went outside.

When she gathered the pieces up there was a crack in her voice but she didn't complain. She assembled it and put the pieces on the very top shelf out of reach. Then she got it into her head that there was someone outside the window waiting to shoot her. She couldn't budge. She went rigid. She sat in the chair, the only time she sat for long, and brought her feet up under her. She was petrified.

When your father came back she told him and he said that was her imagination. She said it was something. He said he wouldn't have wished it over the blooming platter, knowing it was of sentimental value. They must have bought it together. She said to let it. She was overjoyed that he had come back sober.

He had gone to hear Lord Haw Haw on someone else's wireless. Lord Haw Haw was for Hitler, inflaming people to fight. Your father said the Germans were making great strides and that the Jerry was a clever bloke and would win the war.

Next day when the teacher asked girls what their mothers suffered from some said headaches, some said lumbago, some said varicose veins and you were going to say imagination when the Melody one blurted out Piles and Miss Davitt who was laughing up to then took a swipe at one of her plaits and sent her outside. She went down to the closets and didn't come back. Lena Sheedy was sent down after her and didn't come back either.

The closets got scrubbed once a month. Girls did it in pairs, the way girls did a holy hour in pairs. Only the floor got scrubbed. The seats were crusted over. The wood was unrecognizable underneath. There was gray wood and red wood and yellow wood and blond. Arbutus was the most prized wood of all. Mahogany was next. You had six dining-room chairs and a carving chair, all mahogany except for the seating which was leather. In the new plantation there was pine wood, Christmas trees, all the same height and the same color, a graveyard green. The old woods were manifold, treacherous in winter when boughs blew and stagnant on a summer's day. Ambie went down there to shoot snipe and fell asleep and dreamed of being borne aloft on a hammock with crowds cheering. The green got into his vision. The woods created inertia whereas the seaside created vigor.

At the seaside you ran about, splashed, got pink in the cheeks, tucked your dress up under the elastic of your knickers, and hollered to people a long way off. On your way to the seaside you visited a woman. She was a hunchback and wore silver shoes, nighttime shoes. You were with your mother and father and your Aunt Bride. The woman had oysters. She caught them by putting a furze bush in the sand when the tide was out, then when the tide came in the oysters affixed themselves to the thorns of the bush along with seaweed and other addenda.

You were given an oyster as a great treat. It would not go down. It was too big for your swallow. It was both cumbersome and slippery. It was a delicacy. Your father said that was the last time they would bring you anywhere. Your mother said to leave you alone.

The women brought you into the bedroom that led off the kitchen and while you were vomiting your father called in to know if it was vomiting you were. You stooped over a green bucket that had a lid on it. The lid had a basketed button in the center for lifting it on and off. There was a space under the button so that anything could slide through. They peed without lifting the lid. Your mother said all the old things were going out of fashion. The woman ran with the bucket to empty it in the sea. The tide was on its way out. She had to follow it. The sea had left its image on the sand, a purple memory. The wind got underneath and made the grains shift, each grain shifted separately. The other time you saw sand minutely was in an egg timer. It was a way of watching time pass.

She swished the bucket in the water and then threw the contents a long way off, ahead of the spray. She told you to suck a tomato if ever you felt sick. There were no tomatoes to be had. Her upper lip was yellow from smoking. She admired your coat. It was a tweed coat with a flared skirt. It had six buttons down the front.

In summer you left the buttons open. It was your Sunday coat. You wore it to Mass on Sundays, and to Confession on

Saturdays. You went to the curate because the parish priest was deaf and the sins had to be shouted at him. The same set of sins every week. I cursed, I told lies, I had bad thoughts. You sang dumb about the biggest sin of all, sitting on the carving chair in the front room and opening your legs a bit and putting the soft velvet paw of a boy doll in there, squeezing with all your might and then when the needles of pleasure came getting furious with him and chastising him and throwing him face down on the floor with his legs and his jockey's cap any old way.

Afterwards you dusted, furniture, artificial flowers and his toe, just in case. When the priest inquired into the bad thoughts you didn't divulge, but when he gave you a stiff penance like a whole Rosary you thought he must know something. Always before going into Confession your breathing got quick.

Emma fainted once just after she went in and the door flew open and Emma thudded out and her prayer book and holy pictures scattered ahead of her. Hunger some said. Others said cold, because there was no heat in the chapel except that given off by the candles lit for special intentions. Lizzie said Emma had been paying too much attention to her fingernails, buffering them on the back of her fur-backed gloves that were a present from a man she had jilted. At any rate Emma fainted and was carried out. You thought maybe she fainted out of fright but you never said.

After they thanked the woman for the tea and the oysters you set out again and when you got to where there was a strand and some changing rooms you got out because that was the place you had come to see. Your father rolled up the legs of his trousers and paddled. His shins were very white.

Your mother said if he'd brought a cake of soap he could have had a footbath, killed two birds with the one shot. You all laughed. You bought two paper bags of periwinkles and you sat around to eat them, you formed a circle. You were squatting. You had only one pin between the four of you. There was a knack in doing it. You had to lift the little shell off and then unwind the periwinkle very carefully so that it didn't break. They had the taste of the smell of the sea. They made you thirsty. You asked for lemonade. You all had lemonade including your father. The sun came in fits and starts. The periwinkles were the color of hen dirt. You thought that but didn't say so. And you didn't get sick in the car either and neither did your mother or your Aunt Bride get sick. Your Aunt Bride was very excited and kept looking at all the attractions such as the shells and the rocks and the two changing rooms and kept saying Glory be to the great God, today and tonight if it isn't a shell, if it isn't a rock, if it isn't a changing room, and your mother kept replying in a very restrained voice, hoping that your aunt would take the hint and lower hers. Your aunt had a silver brooch in the V of her neck and inside her dress below the V, she kept her powder puff. Every so often she dabbed her face. The powder smelted nice but the puff was mauve and threadbare, like a tongue.

Sandwiches were passed around and when she was gathering up your mother asked who hadn't had an egg because there was an egg sandwich to spare. Your father said he'd rather have a mixed grill and your mother said that was all right for people who had money to burn. The driver sat with you, but not in your circle. You all laughed because of the way he wolfed his food. He put a full sandwich at a time into his mouth and nothing was visible only the fawn crust between his parted lips. Your mother pretended you were laughing at something else, something from the past. Your aunt said it was a memorable day and would be memorable for all eternity. She told about pink birds who crashed against the wind-screens of cars in Italy and who when dead were served on toast. She had read it in a book.

Your aunt was a bookworm. That was what the priest called her, she wormed her way into books. She even read when she was driving the pony and trap, let the reins go slack and gave herself up to reading. She read at night and then made cornflour to cheer herself up. She was not a good cook. The cornflour never had the same consistency, sometimes it was lumpy, sometimes it was runny, and when she burned it she made amends by adding an excess of vanilla essence.

On the way home from the seaside it was milking time and the car had to slow down again and again because the cows were being brought in. Your father went into a pub for a glass of water and your mother sent you in after him. He asked for an aspirin for his headache. The owner of the pub was famous because he had found a collar of gold in a field one day when he was hunting rabbits. He gave it to a museum. You were let shake hands with him. There were men drinking egg flips. There was egg flip on a man's beard and all over his lips, like spit only yellower. Your father had a glass of water, as promised.

You had to pass your own gates to go to your aunt's. That was the arrangement, you would all go to your aunt's for tea. Your aunt lived up the mountains and the higher you went the better the view when you looked back. You were driving

away from the lake that was named after the King of the Red
Eye, a king so generous that he gave his eye away and when
he did he bled a lake from the socket. It was not red though
but gray like the sky itself.

Calves and pigs met her at the gate and your aunt fussed
over them and pulled their ears and though she didn't comment you knew that your mother considered it the height of
sentimentality. You asked if there were tomatoes for tea.

Your aunt had grown tomatoes once and they were put to
ripen on the window sill and had to be turned around and
around, a fraction each day, so that they got uniformly red.
But no matter how red they got the greenness showed
through and they were tart when you bit them. The home-
grown tomatoes were her pride, as were the patchwork quilt
and her garden. The quilt was made up of diagonals and
joins of color and most days she had not time to make her
bed but drew the quilt over it for appearance sake. She went
in for pastel flowers. She liked a garden to look faded, not to
look blooming. The things she detested were begonias.
When you ran your thumb and forefinger along the stalks of
delphiniums the petals fell easily away, flaked, like snow-
flakes only they were blue. Blue was her favorite color. Her
good coat was blue and so was her trousseau when she got
married.

She said it was the wrong season for tomatoes but that
there were lots of dainties. Your father said she should not
have bothered, that a cup of tea would have done and she
said who had been craving for a mixed grill a short time previous to that. He hummed and raised his chair so that the
two front legs were above the floor in such a way that a cat
or a hand could get trapped under them.

You sat in the parlor while she laid the table. She wouldn't let anyone help. Your mother sat on the horsehair sofa and said hairs were persecuting her. It was a cold room and the things were mildewed. There was a photograph of Daniel O'Connell over the fireplace.

From the kitchen you could hear your aunt singing. She sang The Croppy Boy. You recalled the day that she sang when she was churning and forgot her labors and forgot everything so that the butter was nearing cement. She kept coming in and out, first for the cloth, then for the napkins, then for the teapot. Your mother said it would be better to use the everyday teapot that was already nicely lined with tannin, said it in a whisper after your aunt went out of the room. You were all dying for a cup of tea.

Your father asked you when Daniel O'Connell was born and what was his greatest achievement. You rattled it off. Seventeen seventy-five and Catholic Emancipation. Your aunt said that was one of her favorite pictures but your mother said she was not stuck on it as it was too pugnacious. Your mother liked pictures of Spanish ladies in tiered dresses and pictures of Christ. When she lifted the heavy curtain to look out at the lake she said she could not stand the sight of water day in and day out. She said it was one thing to go to the seaside but it was quite another to be confronted by such a vista, eternally. She did not say why. Your aunt announced supper. She put on a funny accent.

It was in the kitchen. The first thing your mother did was warm her shins by the fire. Through her stockings her veins bulged. They were lisle stockings, and she had to be careful of the sparks. Stockings were hard to get and there was no draper friend to her the way Manny Parker's sister was friend and favored her by giving extra chocolate.

There was cold chicken and potato stuffing. The butter

was in fancy pats and the glass dish was laid into cold water. It wobbled. Your mother brought her nostrils near to it and then drew back making a face. Your aunt put heaps on each plate. The stuffing was like a sauce and it spewed over the cold meat. There were hot turnips but everything else was cold. Mixum-gatherum your aunt said. She was delighted to see everyone eating. She took extra bits of meat in her hand and put them on your father's plate. From the steam of the kettle the face powder had gone in crusts all over her cheeks. She felt the material of your father's new suit and said it was worsted, and good worsted at that.

The tailor had made it. The tailor had a game leg and when he measured ladies he touched their diddies. He chalked the shape of the suit out before he cut it. Most men went in for blue serge suits but not your father. Your father preferred brown. Ambie said that cripples were more partial to women than ordinary men and that was why the tailor had an urge to touch girls' diddies. His wife had a brass weighing scales and allowed people to weigh their turkeys, and their suitcases, on it.

All of a sudden your mother began to laugh. She said that when she was in Coney Island a fortune teller advised her never to marry a good-looking man because in that way she would never run the risk of losing him. She could not stop laughing. Your father said what got into her. Your aunt said to your mother that wasn't it so that the first night she got to America hadn't they put her on Ellis Island. Your mother's face contorted and she said absolutely. She said she would never forget it. She described her feelings, how she thought she was going to be exiled there forever. You butted in and said Like Napoleon. You knew that Napoleon was christened the Little Corporal and had a demanding wife called Josephine and had been exiled toward the end of his life. They praised you for knowing that. The way your mother shivered made everyone else shiver. You asked what it was like on Ellis Island. She said terrible. Like the Tower of Babel she said. But the Tower of Babel was somewhere none of you had been to. She said all languages were spoken, divers tongues, mixed in together. She said she was in a bunk with people above her and below her, all talking, all crying. Your father said wasn't it a pity she didn't stay there and enumerated the misfortunes that he would have been saved. But he didn't mean it. Your aunt ladled cream into the glass dishes where she had already stacked mounds of green jelly. Your mother said no cream for her. Like the butter, it had a strong smell. You did not fancy it but you did not say so. Your father congratulated your aunt, said what a spread it was, and she used that moment to tell him how she would always be grateful to him for introducing her to such a good solicitor.

Your aunt liked your father. Your aunt had loved her husband. She believed in love, unlike your mother, who said it was a form of dope. Your aunt called her dead husband her partner. He was shot by the Tans in another part of the country, in broad daylight. When she got the wire she rushed off in a train to get his body and bring him home but when she got there they had already sent the coffin on another train and she was three days at various railway stations trying to locate him. There were quite a few coffins in those days, what with the shooting, and the ambushes. He was buried in the family grave where the bullocks grazed, the island where you would all be buried, eventually. Your aunt had kept a photo of him in the gold locket which she wore around her neck. You asked her to open it. She opened it with her thumbnail and the two discs of gold split in half. He had a mustache. When she looked at him he seemed to be looking straight back at her and he seemed to be saying something or repeating something that he had said before. That was true love, that was, the way your aunt looked into her dead husband's face and conversed with him.

Your mother said did they hear that one about the girl who went to a party and when asked if she wanted any more food, said I have eaten to my satisfaction and if I ate any more I'd go flippety floppety. You helped your aunt to do the dishes. Your mother then said they must take you home because you had school in the morning. Your aunt said it was the end of a perfect day. Your father said Emma would be home soon and your aunt promised to visit. Your mother said it was a promise she hoped would be abided by. Your aunt and your mother kissed and you thought of Mary Magdalene and her sister Martha and how one was a saint and one was a sinner, and then you thought of you and Emma.

There was a surprise at school. Jewel told you that the teacher was going to the loony bin. Told you in confidence. Told all the senior girls. Jewel had it from her mother, where the teacher had gone and borrowed a bedjacket.

Jewel was the teacher's pet the way you were your mother's. She said it was not the public place where all the mohawks went, but a paid place with flowers and an artificial lake. Miss Davitt must have shown photos of it. Miss Davitt told the class that she was going to the city to take a postgraduate course but by then everyone knew and there were sniggers. Jewel offered aloud to go to her house and make a fire and Miss Davitt was thrilled and said Home

Sweet Home and Bless This House. She had books that she did not want to allow go moldy from damp.

She had a new tube of toothpaste, a toothbrush, and a facecloth that was like a mitten. The toothpaste she said was probably of Greek origin like all civilized things. She said what bostoons you all were to know no Latin and no Greek, to settle for a puny alien tongue, to kowtow to the invader. She squeezed a bit onto her finger and ate it. Everyone laughed. Lena Sheedy said that the chimney sweeper had such white teeth because he cleaned them with soot. Someone else said his teeth looked to be white because his face was black, in contrast. A lot of people sided with that. Then someone said that the black doctor would be out from jail soon. The black doctor extracted teeth and got prosecuted because one man he removed the teeth of died from a hemorrhage.

The man who died was Mulligan. The local paper had it —Black Doctor jailed for extracting molars from the mouth of Mulligan. You said it aloud for fun and everyone screamed and then all of a sudden Miss Davitt got very cross and started thumping the girls in the front row and hit the desk with the metal edge of a ruler and told everyone to write out a composition entitled A Day in the Life of a Penny. The girl next to you said to you not to dare rise her again because she might get in a fit and froth from the mouth or do anything.

There wasn't ink in all the inkwells and when girls reached over to dip their pens you could smell them. They all had different smells and along with that each girl had three lots of smell—skin, hair, and clothing. The girls from the town were presentable.

You were finished early but kept your head down. The

poison that had been put out for rats was still there, in corners on crusts of bread. There were different noises, the nibs
of pens that divided in two made a scraping sound, and the
nibs that were drowned in ink made another sound and the
infants ring-ring-o-rosied from the yard.

They were out there unattended. They might come to any
catastrophe, fall into the lavatory hole or get stung, or eat
some weed that was poison, mistaking it for sorrel. The big
girls ate sorrel and sucked the stalks of honeysuckle but infants didn't know one plant from another.

The sums from the day before were not completely
rubbed out on the blackboard. The girl who had charge of
the blackboard was small and could not reach to the top.
The board was on the two highest pegs because Miss Davitt
was nearly six foot tall. Her stockings would not stay up because she had spindles for legs.

When you gave her the bundle of copy books she said
Pray, what are these? and then she started flinging them in all
directions. Some were parted from their covers. Then she
pointed to a spot on the gray cloth map and said that was
where Bally James Duff was before it went bust and then she
doubled over laughing. She said she was already dead. She
composed her epitaph. She said Hail life, sweetness, and
hope and the sooner the better. To thee do we cry poor banished children of Lir, Heaven, Hell, and shingles, Ulster,
Munster, Leinster, and Connaught, asses and gennets when
the cat is out the mouse can play and the Red Branch
Knights doffing their pants in a quiet watered room.

She stood in front of the fireplace and hitched her dress
up to warm the backs of her legs and stayed still like that
until lunchtime. There was no fire on. You all got sent home
early.

Your father told you to go down and see if the horse he
had backed got a win or a place. He sent you down to ask
Lizzie because your own wireless had conked out. Your
mother said it was his own fault for not making sure of the
wet battery.

You ran the first part. Your chest piped. You slowed down.
The grass was warm. The cropped grass was like a carpet.
The high stalks danced and waved. You danced with them.
You touched them. That was your way of saying hello. Yellow flowers predominated. Yellow flowers were your favorites, the warm bells and the warm discs. The dandelions
were bowed down with seed. You consulted one to know the
time. The bits of fluff went in all directions, parachuted,
then dropped, adding to that crop. A weed with very thin
tendrils got itself entwined in sturdier things. You broke
some to make bracelets.

When you passed your throne you sat because that was
for good luck. Every time you passed it you had to sit. Sometimes to avoid it you made a detour. It was a tree stump, a
seat of happiness with briars around it. You had a place trampled down for your feet. Elsewhere the briars flourished,
were its garland. Birds called to each other in the grass. Some
were melodious, some were not. There was whirring, that
was grasshoppers. Chickens screeched. You could hear them
before you could see them. They were submerged in the high
grass.

They were from an incubator and the mother that she had
allotted to them had disdain for them. You ushered them out
to where the grass was low so that they could be on their
guard against weasels. The singing birds did not bother to
fly, they simply walked from one bush to the next. The crows
were on their usual peregrinations, cawing and crying. The

high grass, the low grass, the crows flying, always the same things.

The cuckoo was due. No one had heard it yet. Manny Parker was always first with that tiding. You ran to make up for lost time.

All of a sudden you saw a banana without its skin, on the ground under the outer spread of a tree. You backed away from it. It was slightly rotting. You ran back to tell, kept repeating it before you got there at all, Quick quick, a banana, a banana.

Bananas were phenomena. Scarcely any consignments came from foreign countries and when they did, people were rabid to get them and only city people got them because of being near the docks. There were young children who had never seen bananas at all, only in photos in a geographic magazine.

He and she hurried down. No cows had had the opportunity to lick it because they had been moved to another field that day, since there was a man supposed to have come to scythe the ragwort. The field was deserted except for the hosts of flies who drowsed in the cowpats. They were so still they looked to be dead.

The three of you stared at it. There was conjecture, as to if it was supernatural. All of a sudden she began to laugh, said she knew, she knew how it came to be there. Your father was not bucking any more. He asked her to explain, to elucidate. She said the red-haired tinker had come and since she had two saucepans with leaks and he appeared sober, she had availed of his services and paid him threepence in coppers. Normally she paid him with bread and butter. She reckoned that he must have been given the banana, or he must have stolen it, elsewhere on his travels, and since he had the hungry grass, and got no bread and butter, he was driven to eat it, but didn't know how. She said aborigines were on the increase. She said he'd have trouble with his number two, trying to digest a thing like a banana skin. It was not like her to be crude. Your father said you would all go to the Wattles and the three of you linked, with you in the middle. The sky and the earth had no division and it was like walking toward heaven, with your mother and father and you linked and laughing.

When he lifted the latch Lizzie met him with a glare and said Your horse stood up to shit and he's shitting still. And your mother had to sit down she laughed so strenuously. Then he told about the banana and they couldn't decide which was funnier, the tinker swallowing the skin or Lizzie's remark about the horse that stood up.

Lizzie's parents were at either end of the fire, dazed. Mr. Wattle wore red flannel underneath his shirt and it showed under the cuffs and above the collar. They couldn't know what all the laughing was about because they were deaf.

Your father nodded to them and said to Lizzie How about a cup of tea? She put jam between biscuits to make a sort of sandwich of them. There were holes in the biscuits and the jam came through in little trickles. Every so often he asked her what happened to their horse and she repeated what she had said and the laughing started up again. The two old people munched and kept looking from one to the other of the grownups to try and find out what the amusement was about.

Lizzie walked back with you all to see the banana and your mother said the thing about number two and Lizzie liked that, because she relished a joke and thought of your mother as being a bit ladylike. Your mother picked it up, held it very circumspectly, said there was nothing wrong with it, brought it home and mashed it up with cream and sugar. No one ate it and in the end she was obliged to eat it herself. Your father said once a peasant always a peasant and she cited starving children in war-torn cities and said it was just as well everyone was not so finicky.

When you told about Miss Davitt and her tantrums and her going away he said it was the right place for her as she was always a screw loose. Your mother asked who would be teaching you now and you said a sub but you didn't know her name. The good-looking new guard came with a couple of forms to sign. He brought his melodion. When he was told about the banana he said that red-haired tinker caused more trouble than twenty men and that he ought to be hanged drawn and quartered. She warmed scones in the oven. Now and then the guard unbuttoned the melodion and played a little tune softly. He and your father discussed the case of a shop assistant who had embezzled money.

The guard knew all the scandals for miles around. He said that the two incidents of foot-and-mouth disease had come about because a man squeezed the germ in a hayshed, a man from England. Your mother said she could guess who. They didn't mention names but you knew it was the bald man that bought a mansion for three thousand pounds and had it knocked to the ground and then sold the stones to the County Council for a pittance. He got engaged to a girl from the parish but it transpired he had another wife in England and the girl had to sue him for breach of promise. Your father said he should be run out of the country, what with knocking mansions and bringing in the foot-and-mouth. The guard said he would be, once they had something on him but it was hard to catch a rich bastard like that. The guard said money was a buffer.

Ambie rushed in and said did they hear the news and the more they said no the more he delayed telling it. Miss Davitt had jumped out of the car when they got to the place, pretending that she was about to vomit and had waded into the lake and drowned herself.

Your mother said The Lord have Mercy and your father said Miss Davitt was a nice creature and how they always had a good chat whenever they met. The guard folded the concertina and put it in its case.

Your mother asked Ambie for particulars. He said all he knew was that when they got there she jumped in, clothes and all. She was wearing a brown coat with an astrakhan collar. You had seen her in it. It was nearly a waltz the way she careened to the car. Then she turned around and waved to the school building, viciously shook her fist at it.

Ambie said it was all planned because a cousin had seen her stuffing stones in her pocket but hadn't caught on. Your mother said mad people often showed an amazing cunning and that was the most frightening thing about them. The guard asked what about her house, he was looking for a place to rent so that he could bring his young wife and son from the city. Your mother said most likely it would go to cousins and your father said what cousins because he wanted to cheer the guard up about the prospects of renting the house.

Miss Davitt got a Christian burial after all. For two days while she lay in the mortuary it was feared she might have to be buried in the pauper's grave where there was only a yew tree and a few anonymous people who had strayed into the county and died. All the parents put their signatures to a letter and the doctor brought it to the parish priest who in turn went to the bishop and the upshot was she was brought home but she was not laid out in a bed because for one thing the water had disfigured her.

The crux of the argument had been that she put the stones in her pocket and therefore engineered her death. The woman who cooked for her said she had sent coupons and money away for a little card table and reasoned that no woman contemplating suicide would embark on such a step. That pulled heavily in her defense. She had often uttered the name of that lake when pointing out the lakes rivers and estuaries of each county.

Once she nearly conceded to you when you gave her a very well-done pancake and while you were squeezing the lemon juice on it she fondled the back of your leg the way she fondled girls' legs when she liked them, but it did not lead to an allegiance. Soon after that she borrowed your doll for the school play and never gave it back but kept it in the china cabinet where you could see it, your favorite doll with the high cheekbones and the satin dress.

The school children marched in twos behind the coffin and the twins who were wearing red pixies were asked to remove them by the sub who thought the color inappropriate. You could only walk halfway because you had to go and keep Della company being as she got panic-striken when her mother went to funerals.

Della had consumption and all her brothers and sisters had consumption and had died from it. Hers was not galloping yet but it was obvious she was fading away even though she had egg flips and milk to offset it. After each death they had to whitewash the room and boil the bed-clothes but the germs came back. She called down from upstairs to know if it was you and you knew by her voice she was happy.

She was sitting up in bed very excited. Sometimes she was vivacious and at other times limp, like a weed that had been scythed. She asked if you'd brought any photos of the stars. You cadged photos of film stars from the men who smoked. She had a big array wedged into the front of the mirror over the fireplace. It was in a cane frame and the glass was blotchy. She couldn't touch them with her hand without getting out of bed but she had a feather duster on the end of a bit of bamboo and she used to point to them and dust their faces and have conversations with them.

Her two favorites were Clark Gable and Robert Donat. She was jealous of the female stars and used to be vying with them for the love of Clark Gable and Robert Donat. You had brought her another of Clark Gable, front face, exactly like the ones she had and she kissed it before giving it to you to wedge into place. The way it was now there were more photos than mirror but it didn't matter because she had a little vanity box with a built-in mirror that she consulted all the time.

Beside her bed under a piece of wickerwork was a plastic egg and when she pressed the wickerwork the egg split in half and a very yellow chicken popped up, screeching. It made her laugh and also was her indication that she needed an egg. You went downstairs for one. She asked if you thought Clark Gable was nice to women or a bully. She asked which you preferred in a man, character or personality. She did not wait for a reply to any of these questions.

When you brought the brown egg she cracked it on the

rungs of the bed and swallowed it. She believed they were better that way than beaten with a fork. You sat on the bed and held each other's hands and studied each other's nails. She said there were more white specks on your nails than hers which meant you were less healthy. The pupils of her eyes were huge and the thin rim of color around them a fiery yellow.

She said she would tell you a secret if you promised not to tell. She said the bank clerk was in love with her and had written her love letters. She said the bank clerk admitted in one of those letters that she was the bane of his life. She didn't say how the letters got to her and you didn't inquire because you knew it was a fib.

Then she got you to take down the dress length that someone had sent her and drape it around her. As always you discussed what make it should be. She said she was not going to the tailor, not only because he touched girls' diddies but because he would want to make it into a twopiece and she wanted a dress. The tailor was very hot on making twopieces because he had secured a pattern for that. She draped the material over her head and shoulders and in that pose she looked like the Blessed Virgin. You told her so. Then all of a sudden she jogged up and down and said The game, the game.

The game was to have conversations with each of the film stars, and to make lots of intrigues between them and her.

Clark Gable was the first to speak. He asked her why she went motoring with Robert Donat. She said she liked Robert Donat's car. His car was a Peugeot because Hilda, the richest woman in the neighborhood, had such a car. Then Clark Gable said he'd box her ears if she ever did that again.

She said to Clark Gable What about Dorothy Lamour then, what about her. He said Dorothy Lamour was just a bon-bon compared with her, Della, and then he asked her if she loved him and she shrugged and said she didn't know and when he pressed for an answer she said A teeny bit. Then he took her wrists and squeezed them very tight and she pleaded for mercy and he would not let go until she kissed him and the kiss was on the lips and very passionate. You knew it was passionate because you were Clark Gable and Robert Donat and Dorothy Lamour and all of those charac-ters. You had to take stances on the window sill and do sword fights and use different attire and use different props. When her father came in from work and found you were wearing his good hat and coat he told you to be off, to va-moose, to be out of there. The way he chased you was the way he would chase a stray dog.

When you got home there was a row in full swing. She was frying rashers and the fat had water in it because there was spitting and hissing from the pan. She sent you upstairs for her apron. You hated going up, didn't know what you might meet, Miss Davitt for one thing. She told you where to find the apron and you put your hand in and felt for it on the back of the door but it wasn't there. You had to go in. You prayed

Oh sacred heart of Jesus,
I place all my trust in you.
Mother of God remember me,
St. Anthony pray for us.

The wardrobe door was open, always opening of its own accord as if there was something in there struggling to get

out. The tassel of the blind rattled against the inside of the
window and the rain beat on the outside, the beat of the rain
softer far than the clatter of the tassel. The dark window was
mottled with the rain and trees were huge shapes making
noise beyond the window in the dark. The leaves made one
kind of noise and the boughs made another. You wished she
and you could abscond to somewhere, anywhere. The apron
was at the end of the bed. She did not even notice herself
putting it on so caught up was she in the proceedings. It was
about horses. She said not a meadow existed without useless
thoroughbreds strutting around it.

Your father had racehorses and hunters and hacks. They
were nearly all roan in color but they had different birth-
marks that distinguished them. Before a foal was born he
watched with the mother. Sometimes the mother kicked and
jerked the way a woman would. Afterwards he always gave
her a nice feed of linseed meal and she then stood up and
licked the foal of its moisture, that was like gum.

Your mother pointed out, and not for the first time, that
a horse ate three times the amount of a bullock or a cow. He
told her to mind her own business, to keep her gob shut, to
stick the bacon up her arse.

She said she had rights too, in law. She mentioned the
dowry that her parents had sacrificed to give him.

Her dowry he said did not cover the cost of the hall door
steps. In fact it was one step of dark blue slate and there had
to be salt shook on it in the frost.

Bad language shot out of his mouth, words like shit and
shite, and scutter and arse and arsehole and scour. His language was one thing, his voice was another. His voice was
fierce, like a stone-crusher bearing down on her.

He took the ash plant from its place in the corner and took a few swipes at the dresser. It made a noise like wind and cleft the air. The plates shook. The lids of cans flew about. There were always more lids than cans because the cans were on loan to the people she sent milk to.

She said couldn't he wait at least until the child was out of the way, at school, or at Confession or in bed. He said he bloody couldn't. He gave a few more pelts to the dresser, dropped the stick and put on his hat. A dangerous move. It meant he was going out.

She lapsed into sobs, said he could have all the horses he wanted, as all she was trying to do was to make ends meet.

He said he took her out of a bog and gave her status and would she for Christ's sake recognize the damage she was doing to his craw and his ulcer with her tantrums and her parsimony.

She hung her head and sobbed. She would have taken any insult then because she did not want him to go out. She begged of him to sit and have his supper. He said his supper was ruined.

He sat with his hat on. She added a spoutful of tea to the fat in the pan to make gravy, then poured it on his plate. The moment he began to eat he told you to eat. You said you weren't hungry. He said Eat your supper. You said Yes.

He said you wouldn't get a fry like that in every house. He said did you realize what a good cook your mother was. You said Yes.

You began to recite I wandered lonely as a cloud, as entertainment. He said For Christ's sake to shut up. Your mother signaled to you, then gave a second signal, for you to apologize. One of her eyebrows had got burned from the fat and the speck of black made you incline to reach up and wipe it away.

When you put the bit of egg on your tongue you waited for it to slide down of its own accord, without touching it with your teeth. You were adept at it because of so many Holy Communions. You imagined you heard the sanctus bell and closed your eyes and thumped your breast.

Your father asked why the theatrics and why could you not be a solace to your parents the way some youngsters were. You promised to turn over a new leaf, then jumped up to get the second cup of tea that he was on the point of needing.

When Ambie came in with the two buckets of milk he took stock of the situation quickly and began to hum. The grease had formed a small crust on his egg but it was simple to crack, like cracking very thin ice, one jab of the fork did it. He was wanton with the relish, poured some into the egg yolk and ground the two together.

She burped and put her hand to her mouth, she couldn't stand eggs although they were her livelihood. Six or seven times a day she went to collect them, in the nests proper, and in the bushes because some hens preferred to lay out, in secret. The span of her hand was such that she could take four hen eggs in each palm, four hen eggs or two goose eggs. The eggs that had no shells were funny to hold but hardest of all to crack. It was like a bladder, the outside skin of the shell-less egg. Those that were smeared with dung she cleaned by applying bread soda. She said washing caused them to rot or at any rate hastened the rot. In the spring there was a speck of blood in the egg white, in the mating season. The hens were a breed from the island of Rhodes. They had reddish brown feathers and they had little combs in imitation of cocks' combs. She lifted the clumps of soggy hay out, put the clean dry sops in and shaped them to the nest's proportions. She did it regularly.

With the egg money she bought the jams and the jellies. In her apron pocket there was a bill for eight pounds four shillings but she had told him that she owed sixteen pounds.

That was a lie. No lie could be lawful or innocent, no motive however good could excuse a lie for a lie was always sinful and bad in itself.

He drained his teacup and announced that he was going to bed. He stood on the far side of the kitchen door, eavesdropping. She almost laughed. In times of trial she laughed but it was a nervous trait and exhilarated nobody. In her matter-of-fact voice she said to Ambie would he kill two cockerels for her in the morning. Your father walked away. You could not hear his footsteps because he crept but you could see the absence of shadow in the crack under the door. Ambie said which cocks. She said he knew well which because she had pointed them out to him the evening before. Ambie said he wasn't a poultry instructor but she refused to be riled. When he took his cap off his knee, put it on, and rose, she asked if he had to go. He said a man owed him a bet and he had to get it then or he'd never get it.

Another lie. When he left the house flickered with danger. All sorts of rumbles emitted and you looked at each other to confirm what you had heard. There was no fire lit. She and you rolled skeins of wool into balls. She rolled them and you held them. In between each one you had to rest your arms. You sat by the stove with the oven door open to let out a bit of heat. Sometimes you put your heels on the floor of the oven and stuck your feet in to warm them but it got too hot too quickly and you had to pull them out again. Raindrops slid down the windowpane. At times one raindrop overtook another making a big double drop that slid to the bottom. The window always seemed to have the same quantity of raindrops sliding down. She asked what desserts you thought there ought to be when Emma came.

She was asking to keep your mind occupied. The odd thing was that although you could hear cars going along the road and in summertime identify voices you never heard them coming up the avenue unless you happened to be looking out the front window. The first evidence of a visitor was if the dogs began to go mad.

The minute she heard the barking she pulled off her apron and used her tortoiseshell sidecomb to do her hair. From the rain the back door had swollen and you heard Hilda before you saw her because they had to coax the door, one pushing and one pulling and your mother apologizing and Hilda laughing.

It was a thrill, a visit like that, unexpected, and at that hour. Hilda wore her leopard-skin coat and her hair was in a French pleat. She handed you a cat full of sweets. She had ways and means of getting luxuries like that. It was a black cat, made of cardboard, with ridges in it. They were assorted sweets, some with glassy paper, some with silver paper. You offered them around.

The moment he heard her voice your father must have got up because in no time he was in the kitchen doing up his tie and saying Am I in my own house at all Mister, in imitation of Mr. Wattle. He said what a shame it was not to have had a fire on but due to the funeral they had not got around to it.

He was all pie, admired your cat and said to find him a peppermint. She took Hilda's coat and fitted it on and Hilda said she ought to get one and your mother said she would but in jest. The fur your mother wanted was Persian lamb anyhow. He put on the kettle straight away. Hilda said it was a funny hour to arrive but he interrupted and said she was welcome at any hour of day or night and she was to remember that. Of all the callers she was his favorite.

Some that came were brought to the front room where everyone sat stiffly and struggled to think of topics of conversation, and then later the ladies were brought on a tour of the bedrooms to admire bedspreads and curtains and then they took turns in the lavatory where some peed quietly and some made a great splash. If the lavatory did not flush you told them it was all right, not to persist, that was why you stayed there, to tell them so. So slowly did these entertainments pass that your father always developed a headache and your mother made two if not three rounds of tea.

But with Hilda it was different. Hilda was full of gizz. Your father liked her. When she took up spiritualism he defended her. Hilda had got some books and a special roundtable to try and speak to her dead husband but most people said that as she hadn't spoken a civil word to him when he was alive it was mere hypocrisy trying to talk to him when dead.

She was the richest woman around. Her bathroom led off her bedroom. There was always a mat under the lavatory and a candlewick seat cover that either matched or contrasted with the mat. She had her own electricity plant. Every night there were lights in all the windows and day and night there were batteries charging away quietly and methodically. Her garden was laid out in the form of a Grecian one and between the walks there were heart-shaped flowerbeds. She was noted for her displays of tulips and when they withered they were followed by wallflowers, and she herself said that she had a penchant for wallflowers though her tulips were celebrated. She had a lighter in a gold sachet that she kept flicking on and off even when she was not smoking. Since her husband died she smoked, for her nerves.

Your father said they must go to the races soon. She said def. There were certain words she abbreviated. Definitely was one, and spifflicated was the other. She said spiffo. She herself drank, or as your mother put it, bent the elbow, but she knew when to stop.

Your mother got out the tin of shortbread. Shortbread was Hilda's favorite thing and your mother reserved it for her. Hilda ate two before putting her lips to the tea. She was wearing a black crepe dress and the swoon of her belly was noticeable under it. She kept saying that she ought not to eat any more but your mother pressed her and said she could mortify herself another time. Hilda gave your mother her old clothes and a gift of two pair of silk stockings at Christmastime.

With the eating and the cigarette smoke the kitchen soon got festive. He and Hilda wrangled over whose cigarettes to smoke because they each wanted to wield their generosity over the other. He asked Hilda if he'd ever told her that one about being in the monastery taking the cure, getting up at six for Mass and Matins, getting big breakfasts of rough bread and watery tea but not a drink and how he and Archie Slattery decided to duck away one morning and scrounge a lift to the town. Hilda said to tell it again because it was her favorite story.

He described the frost, the monastery grounds slippy, and the two of them trying to walk away as if it was the most natural thing in the world to be doing. Up on the road he said, there were hardly any cars, because petrol was rationed, there were only creamery cars and bicycles. Not a vehicle, he said to emphasize their plight, and then he described how their hands were cold and their breaths were cold and that it was useless putting their hands in their mouths to warm them. Just when he had built up the bit about the cold he described the car coming around the corner and Archie Slattery nearly throwing himself in front of it. Your mother and Hilda laughed, said he was a scream, said he ought to be on stage. Spurred on by this, he did the accent of the driver who happened to be a Protestant minister, a birdwatcher and a right cod. The Protestant minister refused them a lift because they had come from the monastery and your father described how Archie Slattery soft-soaped him by becoming a turncoat and saying that the monks were a pack of blackguards and a pack of money-grubbing blackguards at that. When they got to the town the first thing they did was to buy a razor and have a shave, then they went to a pub for a few large ones and when they were nicely, Archie Slattery, whose profession was a bacon curer, phoned the local bacon curer and made an appointment for lunch at the Railway Hotel. Over lunch Archie Slattery became Archibald and they all got drunk and then wrangly and the bacon curer sent them back to the monastery in one of his delivery vans that was going in that direction.

He said the monks would have kicked them out except that the prior, who was a friend of his, intervened. But they had their pockets searched and they were relieved of the baby bottles that they had brought back for the thirsty days and nights. The minute he finished, the laughing stopped. It was like turning off the knob of the radio.

They were all quiet, probably thinking how wretched these bouts were. He put his head in his hands and uttered some infant sound and said Never again. Hilda fidgeted with her lighter and said there was a reason why she had come.

Your mother tensed up, thinking it was to demand the money they owed her but it was worse than that. His mare that was at the trainers shied coming out a door, slipped and broke her leg. He looked up stunned and sorrowful and said No. Then he said the mare's name in case there was any mistaking it. She was called Giddy because of her tendencies.

Your mother said in all her born days she had never known two such chancers as those trainers, the Boyce twins who looked identical on purpose so that if you had a crow to pluck with one he could refer you to the other. Thieves, she said, and thick like thieves. He said how was he to know. Hilda said exactly.

Hilda was on his side. Miss Davitt's death she cited as an example of fate. Hilda said they had phoned her about nine o'clock and she had come straight away. She must of course have done her eyelashes and put the French pleat in her hair but she did not mention that. She used olive oil on her lashes to make them glossy. It made her blink in excess.

He thanked her for her trouble. He asked what else they had said. Hilda said that was all she had heard and that the line was bad.

Giddy was brown, so brown that her hide was nearly black and she had come third at a point-to-point on St. Stephen's Day and your father said it was because the course was soggy that she hadn't come first. Her hooves were better on hard ground because he had treated them with vinegar. It was after the excitement of her coming third that he embarked on sending her to a trainer.

He stood up and said he'd better go to her and see how she was. Your mother said what was the use at that hour of night. Hilda said she'd gladly take him but that it seemed fruitless. Your mother said that horse would never see the winning post now. He said what worried him was the loss of her completely, he feared she might have to be shot. Hilda said it might not come to that, it might be a sprain, or a tendon but even as she said it no one believed it.

That night awake or asleep he cried and moaned and from time to time your mother went down and made him a cup of tea and each time when he spoke he said some curse was on him, some blasted curse from antiquity. Your mother said not to talk like that, not to think like that. In the morning he was gone. The thing that you thought would never happen happened.

She left. She put her hens and chickens in the care of Lizzie and everything else she let take care of itself.

Lizzie met you at the gate on her way down from your house. She had eggs in the lap of her apron, which she had gathered up. Your mother would have told her to have them to make up for your keep but to Lizzie that would be a pittance because she liked meat better. She was always hankering after a meat supper.

She said you were to stay with them. She had washed her hair and the tight curls shaped like sausages stuck to her scalp and were secured with grips. She said your mother had left in order to teach your father a lesson. She had gone to her sister, your Aunt Bride. You couldn't go because you had school.

You asked for how long. She said forever if necessary. She said your mother had thought of applying for a job as housekeeper in a holiday camp and you envisaged a cloudless future with your mother and you as caretakers and young children disporting themselves. It was a castle in the air and did not last long. You said what about your sleeping suit. She said your birthday suit would do. She used a lot of slang.

All of a sudden it began to hail and you both ran toward her house. The eggs impeded her running and she harangued because she had just curled her hair. She banged on the door. The old people always locked it when she went out, being scared of tinkers and of the Nigger. Standing by the door you got the biggest ducking of all where the gutter overflowed. They could only turn the key a fraction at a time, it was that stiff. She took her blue telescopic umbrella and went out to examine her snowdrops. Stepping over the low box hedge into the small rectangle of garden she began to coax them. They had fallen down. She knelt and touched them, she tried to make them stand up but no matter what she did they wilted. They were sodden from the impact of the hail and the petals were black from the clay. She told you to go in and get milk.

You hated their milk knowing how Mr. Wattle had allowed the cow to do number two into the pail. She poured one for you. There was dust on it. You thought when she wasn't looking you'd put it into the plant on the window. The plant was mimosa, got to remind her of Australia. She said to stop biting your nails and drink the milk. You said you only drank the milk from your own cows. She said she had never heard such impertinence in all her life. She loved that cow, called her Silky, patted her haunches, often plaited her tail for fun.

It fell dark while you were doing your lessons. You had to draw a map of Europe. You traced it on butter paper and then drew it. That was cheating. The new teacher was stricter than Miss Davitt, but fairer, she had no pets, and no set on anyone. She was called Miss Bugler. When you finished your lessons there was tea and the Rosary. The Wattles retired early. During the Rosary, every time you heard a car you thought it might be your father being brought home and you waited for it to stop or to turn in your gate, and each time when it didn't you murmured a second and a silent prayer in thanksgiving.

But even praying your mind wandered. You thought about your mother and Aunt Bride and what they might be discussing. They never had much to say. Your aunt repeated the love stories she had read or imitated the different bird sounds that she knew whereas your mother liked to dwell on practical matters such as how to make a carragheen souffle or how many ounces of wool were required for a tweedex cardigan.

No sooner were you in bed than you wanted to pee again. Lizzie said Bugger. You were in her bed, on the inside near the wall and you had to crawl out over her. It was a sloping roof and the window was a skylight. Downstairs you stepped into Mr. Wattle's big shoes because they were near the door and you clattered out in the yard to the appointed place where everyone peed day or night. It was as fixed as if it were a lavatory. It had been chosen because dock leaves grew there in plenty in summertime. A couple of drops came. You waited for more, tried to squeeze them out, urged and prayed but in vain. There were dogs barking. You could identify the bark of your own dogs, or you thought you could. The moon was bright and not a soul went by. On your way back through the kitchen Mr. Wattle called from the downstairs bedroom to know who was it and you said it was you and he said to his wife what bug had got into your kidneys because you had been out there no length ago. His wife told him to go to sleep. The red coals buried under the ashes were only raised shapes. You could not see their redness or their glow. You climbed the stairs, skipping the one wooden step that was split, a necessary precaution. You put socks on so that your feet wouldn't freeze hers and getting back into bed you bumped your head because with all the other chain of events you had forgotten about the sloping roof.

Lizzie was crying because of her hair. She had lit the candle and was holding the comb near it. In the wide teeth of the white comb there was a tuft of brown hair. She couldn't stop it falling out and she combed it every few minutes to see how much more she would shed. There were balls of it like balls of knitting wool on the table where she had placed them, to remind herself of her tragedy. You said hair fell out in fits like that. You said it was Nature's way of getting rid of waste. You said your hair used to fall out. You went too far. She recognized the bluff and said maybe you had had jaundice too and a permanent wave. She blamed the permanent wave. She held one ball of hair to the flame for a minute and the smell of scorching reminded you of a chicken being plucked, and brought your mother to your mind. They yelled up to ask if the house was on fire and she yelled down to them to get to sleep and then she winked at you and asked

66

you to do a dummy for her. It meant you were friends.

You were the only one who knew the Melody dummies well enough to imitate their sounds and their slobber. Theirs was the second nicest house in the parish, Hilda's being the first. They also had legacies from relatives in America. The eldest of the Melody brothers who was not a dummy spoke to the other three with fingers and in sign language. You went there every Friday or Saturday bringing the cake of bread that your mother made for them. In return he gave her plums for jam and sugar plums for eating. The cooking plums were black with a dusk on them like a blight, only it was not, it was a bloom. Your mother nearly always included cakes or jam tarts. The dummies went mad for the sweet things.

It was a back road, untarred. In summertime it was dusty and the odd car going by showered dust on the fuchsia. Also it was a terrible road because of the bends. You never knew what to expect, what mad man or mad woman, or motorcar, or animal might be careering around intent on harm. When you were afraid your legs went like spindles and your knees got out of control. The other time when your knees got out of control was when men tickled them to see if you were fond of tea. An auctioneer offered you a shilling once to let him but you said you were too young and ran out of the room.

In one of the fields there was an old bus with two hairy fellows living in it and although they never accosted you, you thought they might. Everyone called them the Hairy Fellows. They left England to escape the war. They were deserters. Your mother said she would love to give them a good wash but your father said it was a kick in the pants they wanted. Manny Parker's sister praised them because they were prompt payers and your mother found that riling. They lived on oatmeal and honey.

The Melodys' house was ornate. It was pebble-dashed with bits of china and glass, mostly dark blue glass, wedged in between the white pebbles. Indoors everything was spick and span, with blossoms or a sprig of green in a jug on the kitchen table, depending on the season. The best cups and saucers were produced for you. The dummies had nice manners but they were always struggling to get their thoughts out and their tongues were slapping and slathering inside their mouths. All sorts of gurgles and noises issued from them. They had hollow cheeks from the exercise and their hands were demented at trying to make sense. They mauled you and kissed you until their speaking brother had to clap his hands and order them to sit down. At first they sat very timid with their hands joined. But then at the sight of the jam tarts they jumped up and grabbed them and fought over them and bit into them as if they had no impediments in their mouths at all. Their chewing was funny.

You did a dummy for Lizzie. You stuck your tongue out, rolled it round and round then let it right back in your throat and made a vomit sound and all the time she kept asking you what you wanted for Christmas. That was what everyone asked the dummies, even when Christmas was ages away. The girl dummy always said a Christmas box. The two male dummies said tobacco, wrote it down. But the girl dummy said it in dummy language. Asked what kind of Christmas box she always said red. Asked what she wanted in the red box she said a box. That was all.

Lizzie laughed and forgot about her hair. Before blowing

out the candle she took a powder. She held the paper above her mouth and allowed the powder to slide in. It was a pink powder and it was for pain. She had pain and was losing weight and that was why she was moody.

You faced the wall and she put her arm around you but it was not like your mother's clasp. You thought it all wrong, you in one bed, your mother in another, Emma in another and your father asleep somewhere, anywhere. maybe on a chair.

The closer Lizzie came to you the more you edged to the wall. It was a damp wall and it smelled like a lime kiln. In her sleep she gnashed her teeth and that was a sign of worms but she was too old to have worms. Through the skylight you could see the moon. It was full and monstrance shaped. The moon seemed to be shining down on you expressly and though you looked back at it you were immune to its magic, thinking only of them.

Your mother sent a dispatch for her Sunday coat, her beads, and a change of underclothes. Ambie fetched them, brought you on the crossbar of the bicycle. Going uphill you both got off and walked. You always gauged his wants, a second before he voiced them. In that way he found you ideal, said he would take you anywhere, around the world on a tandem, a bicycle made for two.

After she'd kissed you your mother asked if you'd been good at school. Ambie brought her letters. One was a repeat of a bill with a red sticker at the end and the other was from the prior of the monastery to say your father was there and doing very nicely. She said Blast it. She said why hadn't Ambie opened the letters and then she could have gone straight home and not had the bother of sending for her

Sunday things. He said how was he to know but that it was a love letter, confidential. They wrangled for a bit.

Your aunt tackled the pony and trap and the three of you set out for home. Ambie went ahead, on his bicycle. Your mother yelled after him to get the stove lit. There was the same moon but you took stock of it now and tried to give it nose and eyes and features, to make it personable. Going up hills your aunt told you to sit back to assist the balance and going downhill she held the reins very taut especially when the pony tried to gallop. Your mother was nervous. You didn't talk much, just saluted people that passed by and commented on the nice night. There was not a puff of wind. It had rained all day and the air was soft and when a match was struck it didn't have to be shielded. Men going by struck matches. The pony farted from time to time and your aunt made a joke, said Beg Pardon on its behalf. When you passed ruins on the road that were supposed to be haunted you blessed yourself and closed your eyes.

You beamed when you got out to open the gate. Your aunt declined an invitation to come up. The line of water that had clung to the spears fell in one swoop and drenched your insteps through your ankle socks. You only opened half of it. When they kissed, your aunt said that she would miss their chats. There was always someone made lonely.

Going up the fields you told your mother about Lizzie's hair falling out and about the medicines she took and your mother put her arm around you and said one's health was everything. She slipped on a little mound of grass and thought she had broken her wrist. One hand was in her pocket, and had taken the brunt of the fall. When you took it out you expected to see it detached but it was all in one piece and even though she yelled when you pressed the various muscles she was laughing and frivoling. It took time to get the stove going. She broke up a butter box. It was like giving someone a tanning the way she put the wood across her knee and used brute force on it. To get the kindling bits she had to resort to the hatchet which she was not enamored of. As soon as she'd put a match to the fire you listened for the draught, listened for that thundering roar, spoke to it, egged it on.

A fly and a flea and a flue
Were in prison so what could they do?
Said the fly let us flee
Said the flea let us fly
So they flew through a flaw in the flue.

It was a grand reunion. Your mother put the hat with the veil on. Your father was tentative, bowed down with mortification, lost for words. He looked at you and said you'd grown and was it so that your hair was a shade lighter. You had treated it to a rinse of camomile flowers to try and induce it to be blond. The older you got the more you aped Emma, you wanted to be blond like Emma, to be a whitehead, to have a watch, to have a cyst, to have a shorthand speed of ninety words per minute.

A monk with a beard received you. He had a brown habit with very spacious pockets. There was nothing in them. They were not gaping. He was in charge of the vegetable garden. It was a policy that a monk or a priest with an aptitude for one thing was obliged to take up another occupation altogether, for humility's sake. You wondered if he had had a beard when he was out in the world or if he had gone to hurling matches and hollered.

Priests passed back and forth, carrying buckets, carrying books and jotters, all in a hurry, all on their way to their respective duties. From a classroom you could hear the chanting of Latin words and you were delighted to be missing school. When one particular priest passed by your father said aloud that he must be the bravest man in the land because he had been singled out from a whole community of brave men to go up and bless the spire of the new church. He pointed. You looked up. It was a stone spire, gray at the bottom, blue where it caught the sun and after that no color at all only a dark shaft of stone in the sky. Scaffolding was still up. The brave priest did not smile or make any acknowledgment of the fact that your father had praised him. He was on silence.

They were all on silence most of the time and you imagined that probably they formed friendships which did not depend on speech, a smile, or a look, or something of their belongings, exchanged. The monk said that the priest had once been a bit of a playboy and was now a luminary to the entire order. He took two strawberries from his big brown pocket. They were joined together by a sprig of green. You held them, not wanting to eat them. Your mother said wasn't it marvelous to be able to grow strawberries in such an inclement country, and the monk said that anything could be done with a bit of patience and application. Your father said it was no longer a question of potatoes and cabbage. The monk said not at all, on the contrary, that with cloches one could be adventurous, nay exotic. You asked what were cloches.

The monk led you across the grounds to the garden gate and when you looked through you saw a long row of little glass houses, in a straight line, with metal girds around them to keep them from breaking. Your father said to tell the honest truth he himself hadn't known what cloches were and wasn't it a good thing you had asked. Your mother gasped, said ignorance was the bane of mankind. She added womankind in case your father might think she was having a dig at him, although they were all smiles and he said sorry if out of forgetfulness he went up a path ahead of her.

The strawberries had stained your hands, made them fragrant and caused black specks to lodge between the folds of your fingers. You ate them. The monk gave him a medal with a saint's face engraved on either side and a booklet with prayers addressed to St. Jude, patron of hopeless cases. He accepted them slavishly, cried. Your mother was reduced to tears. Big slow tears coursed down her cheeks under the veiling and then just in the nick of time she put out her tongue and caught each one and brought it back into her mouth.

They thanked the monk for everything, his prayers, the walk, the strawberries, the opportunity to see the cloches. Your mother left a small offering to be put toward the debt involved in the building of the new chapel. Exalted though she was by the prayers and the tears she got out a pencil and an old envelope and asked the monk to repeat the ingredients and the method for the dessert they had been given after lunch. It was called Charlotte Russe. She said she would call it Finbar Russe in honor of the monk who had made it. The moment the car drove off the monk lowered his head and put his cowl up and you took that to be an indication that he was retreating into silence again. You felt very sorry for him even though his life had all the serenity that your mother and father's lacked.

Your father sat in front and you were in the back next to

your mother and on your other side there was a big cold space where nobody sat. Going around corners you fell on her and going around other corners she fell on you and you both exclaimed and laughed. Your father held the strap that was fitted to the side of the car and asked the driver if he knew what cloches were, asked very cocksure. He was delighted at being able to describe them.

When the car crossed from one county to the next your father knew although it was not written up. He knew the fence or the stone wall, or the tree, or whatever it was that marked the boundary between one county and the next. If there was something in particular that he pointed to, you tried to focus it but your stomach began to sway and your head too and the sway interfered with your vision. Excitement got the better of you. Each time when he said Look, you got dizzy and couldn't see.

The counties were all different. Some had good land and two-story houses. There was one house in particular that caught your fancy. It had creeper on the walls and in the grounds white statues that looked to be made of marble. The driver said that the owner was a dypsomaniac. He said that one of her children had died from a wrong injection and had been buried in the back garden, and that dogs were buried there too and had gravestones. Your mother said that money wasn't everything.

You passed cottages too, and small-holdings and trees of every denomination and walls and ruins and tar barrels bedecked with flags indicating that men were working on the road, although they weren't. Sometimes your father sang a few bars of a song and often stopped abruptly to tell some story about some man in one of the towns you passed through. He knew everything about those towns and their inhabitants and you thought that for a drunk man he had gleaned a lot on his travels. He told stories about men, friends of his, up to mischief, trying to escape for the day from their wives or trying to get in with the gentry and follow the hunt and be served glasses of sherry, before and after, on nippy mornings.

The driver said that in the house with the statues there had been a marquee hired once, for a party and how one of the guests ran his motor car through it for a bet. He said someone's legs got mangled but as far as he knew it was a member of the staff and not a guest. When there was a silence it was not hurtful, it was only that your father was waiting for something else to crop up in his mind. The driver and he were without a match, so they kept smoking, each one taking it in turns. Your father had a nice stock of cigarettes, not having been at home to use his quota for a while. Your mother brought them for him, the six large packets in their yellow boxes with cellophane around them.

When you got into your own county you saw first the lake and on it the island where your family was buried and the littler islands all around. The lake and the road were adjoining. You could see the reeds and the wind rustling them. Some had brown seed pods and some had not. Reeds always looked miserable. You drove through a valley where it was as dark as inside Jacksie's forge. Then you parted from the lake. It was down below, in a dip and miniature. Your mother said if that wasn't panoramic she'd eat her hat. Your father looked at the various haysheds to see what farmers had the hay in. He was not jealous at the fact that some were better husbanders than he.

In the village people gaped, to make certain it was him coming home. The ball alley looked gloomy because there was no one in it. Only on Sundays did it have a crowd. The inside was plastered and ugly whereas the outside was a nice stone, but the inside had to be plastered for the ball to bounce. Lizzie had washed the sleeping suit that she had loaned you. It was on the clothesline flapping back and forth. It was a blue silk pajamas and when she first came home from Australia it was a novelty, it and a case that matched, both of which she showed to people when she was showing her dresses and her shoes and her ermine stole. The wind ballooned the legs and it was like seeing a person with very large thighs on a trapeze seeing it buffet back and forth.

At the first clink of the gate the dogs raced down the field and when they saw your father they got deranged altogether and he had to wind the window down to let them jump up and lick his fingers.

The pencil was so sharp it ate a hole in the page. You were making a list. You wrote the words with a flourish. Raspberry, strawberry, black-currant jam.

She said wait a minute, to remember you weren't skipping. You often skipped to that, raspberry strawberry black-currant jam, tell me the name of my young man, A-B-C-D-E-F-G. You always tripped deliberately at J because you had a hunch that you were going to marry a man called John. After jams you put down lemonade. Then sardines. Then pickles.

She jumped up, countermanding, said there were pickles. They were not individual pickles, not chunks of cauliflower or cucumber that you could identify, but a mush, and a vile shade of yellow. She said the makers were esteemed. He said he'd soon see. He couldn't undo the top and finally had to resort to doing it with the aid of the door. He held the jar between the jamb and the partially opened door, then tried to force the door closed, until she said he would break it. He snarled at her. Summoning up anger. Your novena was that they may never fight again. She took the jar and opened it with her bare hands, the brass spiral flew off. She lifted a speck onto her little finger and asked you to sample it. It was savory. You crossed out pickles, put several lines through it, horizontal, then vertical to make sure it wasn't legible.

She was economizing. She wanted to buy blinds with slats. She had seen them in Hilda's house, had admired them and later in the presence of your father went into raptures over them, said how they would never fade or flitter like the canvas ones she had. They made stripes along the floor, stripes of light and stripes of shadow. You didn't like them, because you couldn't see out properly, the world outside got divided up into sections, the sky got reduced. She was determined to get them, she even voiced the hope that Emma might contribute, that Emma might very well club in for such an innovation. Emma liked the modern things.

The doors of the three downstairs rooms were open and bits of wood wedged in under the window sashes where the cords had gone. In one room there was lemonade, in another a fruit cake, in another cold mutton, all in honor of Emma. You put rhododendrons in a bowl, one big flower in each bowl, one for Emma's bedroom, and one for the room where the tea table would be laid. She said they would wither and have to be thrown out but she was too occupied to be really vexed. They were big and waxy like stars come down to bloom. She was making fillings for sandwich cakes.

In Emma's bedroom the tin of cling peaches was in the cupboard where it had lain for years and years, ever since the music teacher had given it to Emma as a prize. No one had

EDNA O'BRIEN

permission to open it. First thing when she got home Emma always said Are my peaches there? and ran to look and in the bedroom she stood before the oval mirror and touched her hair with a silver-backed brush that was also hers, and which your mother allowed no one else to appropriate. Your mother told Ambie to make certain and sure that the bicycle was in good trim. When Emma came home she went to the village four or five times a day and sometimes for no errand at all. She changed her clothes before each journey and that was why she was called a fashion plate.

In the midst of the preparations the major came to talk about a horse that he was considering for training. When your mother saw his car she groused but your father went down the avenue to meet him which was always an index of a great welcome. The major wore tweed plus-fours and a cap that matched. Your mother said she wasn't interrupting her duties to dance attendance on any major.

Your father brought him to the room where the cake was, and inquired after his wife. The major and his wife were separated but your father always asked how she was. The major's voice reverberated all over the house. He said yes, that as it was such a nice morning he wouldn't be saying no to a drop of paddy, but only a wee drop. Your father called you aside and said to fly for it on the bicycle. He had no money. He told you which pub to go to, the nearest one; a terrible ordeal, because he and the publican were at war over a bill of long duration.

The publican was in his stocking feet when you got there, he kept erratic hours. He was sweeping the floor and had already sprinkled it with tea leaves, to keep the dust down. He was a bachelor. The thing that caught your eye as always was an advertisement for headache pills that showed a woman

80

frowning fearfully and beside it a hand-printed new sign No tick today but free drinks here tomorrow. You took it to pertain to your father, personally. He didn't have to ask what you wanted, he saw the bottle in your hand. Once there had been an iron tonic in it and part of the label remained. He poured the whisky from a big bottle through a paper funnel into the iron tonic bottle. He hadn't bothered to rinse it. You said it was for your mother for a cake. He approved of your mother, said she was like the violet, shy.

You said Emma was coming home. He said Emma must be a woman now. You thought that by a woman he might mean a whole series of personal things; being bosomed, et cetera, things you shied away from. The cork he chose was too small and fell into the whisky bottle. He left it there and got another cork but wrapped paper around it to make it plump. He simply raised one eyebrow when you said could it go down in the book till next week. He was not put out. He asked if you knew that Americans were mining for gold in the other end of the county and you said how you'd read about it and how you'd like to see gold while it was still dust and before it was fashioned into a ring or a brooch. For no reason he said head or hearts and gave you the opportunity of winning sixpence.

It was a bravura ride downhill toward home. The bicycle ran away with you and you came a cropper and crashed into the ancient wall that supported one of your own gates. You screamed. Then squat and spraddled between the front wheel of the bicycle and the seat you steadied yourself and saw that the whisky was intact. You kept a firm grip on it. Luckily none of the Wattles appeared. Your chin and elbow were grazed. It took some time for blood to flow.

Going up the avenue you pushed the bicycle and almost

at once your father came out of doors and waved you on. You dropped the bicycle and ran. From the impact of the drop the spokes pzzzzzzzzzzzed on the grass. He said why hadn't you cycled and you said you didn't know. While he poured the whisky your mother left off from icing the cake, in trepidation as to what might happen. He poured hurriedly and his hand was shaking. The cork in the bottle impeded the flow and he blasted the publican for being so careless. He poured half, looked at it in the glass, then poured the remainder and your mother closed her eyes with relief, knowing that the temptation had passed.

The major was studying the design of the marble fireplace and saying what blinking craft had gone into it. He said it would fetch a nice penny at an auction and your father said what a pity it was a fixture, or it could be sold. You did the daftest thing, you handed your father the sixpence. He said what was that for. You said for overheads. He laughed. The major laughed. He pretended to keep it. He called your mother in to tell her what a generous girl you were and she too was touched and half in sadness and half in happiness she said to the major that between you and your father there was a real bond but that neither of you would ever admit it.

The major said love was a deuced thing. No one knew what he meant, just like when the matron had said that the Nigger's kiss was like a swab. Your father handed you the sixpence and, mortified now, you used the thin edge to push back the skin and give your nails some half moons.

She asked the major to wait for lunch although she had no intention of cooking any. The incident had mellowed her. He said there was nothing he would like better, but that if he wasn't back his cook would never let him hear the end of it.

They were having jugged hare. The major said that a man was as beholden to his cook as to his wife and your father said wasn't it a bind to be bullied by one of your own servants and he made some reference to his nanny, how they used to have to humor her by giving her port wine. The major said apropos of nothing how he liked to take his exercise after lunch to work off the fat and he said there was no better way of seeing the world than from a horse. Your father agreed.

He had rapport with horses but he never rode them. He put ropes round their necks and ran with them to break them in. It was always a rearing affair and your mother used to implore of him to at least do it in the walled garden so that the horse could not campaign too far or too calamitously.

The major and he did not get around to discussing business because the moment he had drained his glass the major said he must be on his way. It was left pending. Your mother was ripping. The dogs chased the car as far as the gate. Your mother rinsed the glass to remove the whisky smell and said to your father why hadn't they got down to brass tacks. The plan was that the major would train the filly and that they would jointly own her. Your father said that not everyone was as precipitate as she and that it took men two or three meetings to measure each other's caliber. Your father added that Rome was not built in a day. Your mother said he was very quick with the proverbs but she was not incensed over it.

In the sunlight the hens' droppings were a startling sight. Forty-three hens had done their different droppings on the flag. You threw buckets of rain water on it then swept it with a coarse brush. Then you cycled up down and around, cycled manically, ringing the bell, taking your hands off the handlebars, squeezing the brakes, anything to pass the time.

When Emma got off the train it was pitch. She said how quiet, how balmy the country air was. The porter looked at her astonished. She had an accent. She told your father that she had been treated to tea and scones on the train by an industrialist. Your father said a man like that was worth knowing, worth cultivating; added that he himself might be needing a bit of farm machinery later on and might be able to get it at cost price through the influence of such a man. Emma made no rejoinder.

In the car you touched her hair, but lightly, so that you were not sure if she felt it. She asked how was mummy. Your mother was at home doing last minute things, slicing the cold meat, distributing the pickle mush, laying serviettes out. A car coming in the opposite direction didn't dim. Emma told the driver not to dim either and was very adamant about it. The headlights of the other car enraged her. A rabbit crouched in the middle of the road and it reminded your father of the major and the jugged hare. Your father said they ought to kill it and bring it home and jug it for your mother. It must have been diseased because it refused to budge and the car had to skirt around it. Each time when you touched her hair you thought of things that you might say to her, such as Hello, or that the bicycle was pumped up or that you had a silk hankie for her.

She got a gala welcome. The new guard was there. Lizzie had put on rouge and even Ambie had deigned to stay in. First thing Emma did after kissing your mother was to pick up the guard's melodion, strap it over her shoulder, and attempt to play. The guard put his fingers over hers and taught her a tune that was all the rage at the time. It was about little holly trees and little babbling brooks and pulled at every-one's heartstrings.

Emma was wearing a black crepe dress and white sandals with wedge heels. The heels were made of cork. She'd got fat. When Lizzie remarked on it Emma was livid, said on the contrary, she had lost weight. Your mother said she didn't want to hear any talk of diets or starvation because every-thing was to be eaten up. Emma was told about Miss Davitt and she impressed everyone by saying that she had seen it in the paper and had already arranged to have a Mass said.

Then your mother asked Lizzie and your father to tell jointly about the horse and the banana but they clashed over the order of the events. Your Aunt Bride described the day at the seaside, the waves, the rock formation, the cries of the birds, plaintive and otherwise, but it was the same as if she was talking to herself because she kept looking down and picking up crumbs on the base of her fingers and dropping them again. Her comments drew no applause from anyone.

Then Emma conducted the conversation. She told how two American soldiers went to an ice-cream parlor in the city and asked for two nice cups of coffee like the sweet Ameri-can girls and was asked by the waitress Black or White, sir?

Ambie applauded that, and your father asked Emma to tell it again and begged of everyone else to shut up. He was very testy and wanted Emma to talk exclusively to him.

Then your father told about Ambie and his friend Jacksie eating a chicken that wasn't drawn and getting sick over in the forge and Lizzie said not at table and burped, but your father went on about how they had tasted bits and enjoyed them immensely but when Jacksie stuck the spoon in to haul out the stuffing, something else altogether shot out in his face—some oats—and the two of them had to run for it to the back of the forge and be sick. The chicken was a gift from a man who had come to have his horse shod.

Emma changed the subject by saying that a head of cabbage varied in price from one shop to another as much as twopence a head and how toward the end of the week she had to go far afield for hers. Your father said what a shame and to think he threw cabbage to the cattle and what a pity he could not send her some. He did not add that it was riddled with holes and it took twelve heads to make a saucepan full and how your mother had to chop it away until she got to the heart where the slugs found it harder to penetrate, the heart being tightly bunched and impenetrable.

Emma called your mother Mummy, and your father Daddy and made frequent use of the other people's first names. You blinked to get attention and your father told you to stop blinking. Emma sent you upstairs for her handbag. In it, there was her diary, leather-bound and with a pencil attached, a small bottle of gin, pearled nail varnish, nail varnish remover and a piece of soiled cotton wool that had traces of lipstick and suntan lotion.

Emma's legs were very brown. In one house that she visited there was a heated swimming pool and spare sets of togs for visitors. At midnight a butler had served hot bouillon, then rashers and eggs. Emma said he had gloves on and your father said that would be the next thing your mother would be doing, putting gloves on to pass pieces of cake. When you got back Lizzie was spanning Emma's waist and saying how she musn't lose her figure. Lizzie's fingers were long, the nails sharp and clayed and it was like seeing antennae trying but failing to enclose Emma's waist.

Hilda who was expected didn't arrive and your father remarked on her handsomeness and there followed a heated argument as to what was the difference between handsome and pretty. Ambie said Dorothy Paget was his idea of beauty and described what gills she had. He had seen her at the races masticating chicken. Ambie and his friend Jacksie cycled to the races every year and stayed in a hotel but didn't leave their shoes out for polishing in case of theft. Your father went too but he was always in a different enclosure where he could be near the horses and chat with the trainers and get tips. Ambie voted for Dorothy Paget and the guard said it was hard to surpass Greer Garson but he knew someone who did and he looked at Emma. Lizzie said everyone was nothing in the end but a heap of flesh and bones and your father said brusquely that that did not take away from Emma's luster.

Your Aunt Bride said that in her estimation both girls were beautiful and your mother said to your father that it wasn't fair to single out one above another and that anyhow beauty was in the eye of the beholder. There were tears in your eyes and hot tears going down the back of your throat which you were endeavoring to swallow. The conversation got stifled.

The guard stood up to leave. Only then was it noticed that the dogs had been indoors all the time, under the table, and they had to be given mutton to lure them out. Bran, the dog named after the chieftain, often refused to go, had to be badgered and often when he got as far as the door and saw the bribe that was awaiting him, the crust of bread, or the bone, or whatever, he returned to his haunt under the table. Your father gave them a kick to usher them down the steps.

The sky was a deep blue and riven with stars. There was a slight breeze and the rustle that the trees always gave. The new guard looked up, said If you could wish upon a star, and went down the steps, floundering. Emma had made another conquest.

In the middle of the night you found her peering down the lavatory bowl with a candle held down to assist her vision. You thought it was an earring she had lost, or a hairpin, or a tooth. My aunt, my aunt, Emma said in a very jubilant voice as she flushed the lavatory. You were afraid she would waken the house. She asked if you knew what she meant, if you were acquainted with the facts of life, and you said yes, but haltingly. Blood flowed from you, came upon you unsuspectingly when you were on a roadside where you had gone to sit and see horses and caravans and animals file past as the traveling circus came into town.

You were able to provide her with the necessary and two large safety pins. Your mother had made the napkins herself, they were big and ungainly, with herringbone stitch in other colors along the hem. They were white. Emma thanked you and closed her bedroom door to be private for a minute while she put it on, then opened it and said to sit by her for a while, to sit and chat, for old time's sake. It was like a song the way Emma worded it. You sat outside the covers with the eiderdown around you.

She said to give her all the latest, the scandals, the summonses and the amatory pursuits. You could only think about Jewel and how she was going to a convent where she would be taught deportment as well as academic things. Emma said in the joint where she went there were dumbbells and barbells but they were only used to put on a display for a bishop whose calls were few and far between. Emma had been to a convent of lesser renown. You told her they were digging for gold in the mountains. She said if they got any to let her know, to let her know anyhow and she giggled.

You touched her toes outside the covers and in one rush all the friendliness that was between you came back and took possession of you and you were her slave. You asked to be told more about the city and the sights. She said she was so popular with bus conductors that she almost never had to pay her fare. You asked if she had a boyfriend and she said hosts. She couldn't wait to get back to the city, she had come home only to please the folks.

This Dump, This Dump she said. The room was an insult, a paper fan in the fireplace, soot behind that, a chair with a broken back, trunks with school books in them, the press where the cling peaches lay, and a fitted wardrobe with two wire hangers for her clothes. She had thrown the bulk of her things over the chair and she promised that next day she would allow you to try them on.

You said that if you could borrow a bicycle the two of you might go down to the lake and sit by the water's edge and paint your nails. Emma said the boatmen going by would take the dangling of your fingers to be hellos, and would come and abduct you away. She took the gin bottle from her bag and said she had proved that for menstrual pains there was nothing to beat it. She let you taste it.

You told her about the major coming and how your father hadn't touched the whisky but Emma did not want confidences like that. She asked how the hot water situation was, because she liked lolling in her bath, in fact she said it was one of her primary pleasures to loll in the bath and with her

89

big toe to keep turning the hot tap on and off. She said the name of the bath oil she used. She described how it made a veneer on the surface of the water and how it had the perfume of the woods. The woods Emma conjured up were not like the ones beyond the window where the old trees reigned and the badgers roamed and the dogs convened at night, Emma's woods were bright and blossomy as in an operetta.

When she fell asleep you folded the sheet back so that the blankets would not tickle her chin and you token-kissed her, you brought your face near enough to be able to feel her breath and then you let your breaths mingle but you did not touch her cheeks or her lips.

You slept it out. You had to miss school. There was sleep in the four corners of your eyes, yellow crystals that you wormed out. They were like grains of sugar between your fingers. Emma called you a little minx, said you had slept it out on purpose. She and you had boiled eggs for breakfast. She ate hers so thoroughly that the inside was as bald as the outside shell. She had eaten the thin skin around the albumen. You didn't do that, you didn't follow suit. Afterwards she forced her spoon through the shell for fun, and you did the same. They were egg spoons, smaller than the teaspoons and they were yellow from years and years of contamination with sulphur.

It was teeming rain. The rain fell perpendicularly and made a sound as of bullets. Your father trod on the spaces between the sheets of newspaper that she had put down to protect the tiles. There was different-colored muck, brown and ocher muck on the soles and up the sides of his heavy boots. He had taken a short cut through a plowed field, did it so as not to be too long absent from Emma and the entertainment of the kitchen.

The water ran down the brim of his hat and down the length of his oilskin coat and created a pool on the floor. A reminder of when the dogs were pups but there was no smell from it, there was no smell attached to rain itself. It brought out the smell of whatever it touched, the fiber of cloth, the darkness of mushrooms, the inner unction of trees. When he removed his hat and coat everything within reach got a ducking. Emma put her hand over her correspondence. He touched her wrist and begged her forgiveness. It was like a gesture in a play. His hat was a very dark brown from the rain and he explained to her that its true color was buff. His hand lingered over hers. She spurned it.

The hens' trough was full of water. It had rained at least two inches. The hens' trough was two inches deep and V-shaped. Your mother tipped it upside down. You helped her scoop out the food, she used a broken garden shovel, you used a lath of wood. Then hens were reluctant to come out of their house. One came, then the cock came, then they all came. They were not discerning, they all convened at one end of the trough leaving masses of untouched food at the other end. The door latch was wet, and overlaid on the wet was gray mash from her hands. The dogs got in. He shouted at you to get them out.

Emma put the letters she had written in her cardboard writing case and tied the two ends of thin ribbon together. You longed to know who she had written to. She used her saucer as an ashtray. She chain-smoked, drank tea with hardly any milk, only a sensation of milk, as she put it. She wound her watch and asked at what time the doctor finished in the dispensary. She said she did not want to go to his house because that would make it into a social occasion. Your mother asked what was it then if not a social occasion.

Emma said she had a little ailment and that she would like a consultation about it. Your father said that if it was her stomach she could use some of his jollops. Sometimes it was thought his ulcer was peptic and sometimes duodenal. The symptoms varied and so did the degree of pain. He even credited himself with having both. Emma said it wasn't digestive trouble and left it at that. She made it clear that she did not want it enlarged upon.

The pools of water on the road were deep and mud-colored and the two times when a car went by the backs of her legs got spattered and she consulted them to see if her suntan lotion had got smudged. She decided to let the spatters dry for fear of harming the beautiful even film of brown. She asked you to say a little prayer for her. She said she might as well tell you what it was being as you were her confidante, it was something to do with the bladder.

You could only think of pigs' bladders and how when he blew air into them and trapped it and bound it with a piece of cotton thread Ambie used them to play football with, until such time as they burst. Bladders were pus color, had a glaze.

You said a dog bit the postman and he was suing the Hairy Fellows, the owners. Anything to get off the subject of bladders. It was a Tibetan dog. You had never seen it. You had heard of it. It was shaggy. In Tibet there were lamas, holy men, but their souls were eternally lost because of the god they worshipped. They had devil dances and barley grew there.

Emma had timed it perfectly. The other patients were gone, and so was the dispensary nurse, a meddlesome woman, who would have insisted on staying behind on the excuse that she had to boil water to sterilize instruments. The doctor was gamey with Emma, said why hadn't anyone told him she was home. Emma said she was home no more than twenty-four hours and there she was at his disposal. He took her arm and conducted her in. You were crouched down behind the wall, directly opposite. Emma had suggested that you hide, said your presence might banjax her position. The moment they went in you brought yourself up, first by kneeling and then by standing. Your knees were pocked from the uneven ground.

There was a smell of night-scented stock in the air. It was from the creamery manager's garden, they were the only people apart from Lizzie that bothered to sow flowers. The lamp was lit again and the plastic half-curtain drawn. He drew it. You saw his small fat hand, the hand that you had seen administer to people in different circumstances. He had attended to you, had syringed your ears and afterwards pulled your earlobe by way of a joke. He was good with ladies, had a bedside manner.

The rain had stopped but everything was wet. The lichen on the wall was revived by rain. Some was raised like a cushion and some had passed into the body of the stone and had become part of it. There was white and green and rust-colored lichen and there were queer shapes, all wavery at the edges, like the borders of countries on the school map. You scratched the stones with the edge of a pebble.

Austria was Hungary
She ate Turkey,
Dipped it in Greece,
Fried it in Japan,
Dropped it in the middle of the Indian Ocean,

While long-legged Italy,
Kicked poor Sicily,
Into the middle of the Mediterranean Sea.

You were tired of sitting and you were tired of standing. After it got dark you coughed when people went by so that they would know you were you and not mistake you for a ghost. People mistook Manny Parker for a ghost because of the way he mooched around at all hours, in the dawn, in the dewtime, gathering different specimens. Your father had a set on Manny Parker and on the Hairy Fellows, pretended he was afraid of them, pretended, so that he could denounce them.

You tried to whistle. Only men should whistle. The Blessed Virgin blushed when women whistled and likewise when women crossed their legs. It intrigued you thinking of the Blessed Virgin having to blush so frequently. The bird that had the most lifelike whistle was the curlew. The curlew was a grallatorial bird, indigenous to sedge and damp places, more partial to wading than flying. The curlew's whistle was a cry.

The light in the dispensary window got quenched but neither of them emerged. You said five Our Fathers and five Hail Marys. Then you said five Glory be to the Fathers. Glory be to the Father was routine, was like the full stop at the end of the words. You said a litany. Behind you there was a field of corn and it was green and vast. You could imagine things looming, animals, a chariot, Miss Davitt. Your prayers got very singsong, and weren't delivered for Emma but were said to keep ghosts and chariots away.

When Emma came out she was vivacious, said what an

angel you were, what a little dote, what a little lapdog. She
said it had taken longer than she had imagined because it involved various tests and what a nuisance it all was, one's insides, the inner paraphernalia of one. Women's insides were
a sea with shapes sliding and colliding and fertility juices
leaking away. She hopped. She frolicked. She did not mind
when her legs got spattered. She was exalted. She said she
was off, in the morning, to take the spa waters for her complaint. It was to a town several hundred feet above sea level.
Elderly people went there when the harvest was in. It had
five or six hotels and many guest houses. She had no idea
where she would stay.

They stiffened when they heard it. Your father said she
was just home and it wasn't a very civil thing to be gallivant-
ing straight away. Your mother said it was a waste of money.
Emma wasn't very flush, had brought no presents, Emma
had hinted about being a bit short of spondulics. Emma said
she must go, that it was a must. She asked what time the bus
went in the morning and grudgingly she was told. All the ju-
bilation had passed. It dawned on them then. Things are
known before they happen.

She tried humoring them, asked about his crops, his pasture, his cattle and his horses; asked how the hens were laying. For fun she plaited your mother's hair and when she
milked each plait like a cow's teat, no one laughed and no
one smiled. He dragged his chair, scraped it along the floor
and stood up and announced that he was going to bed. A
pall had set in. When he had gone your mother asked if it
was really necessary, this jaunt, and Emma said that it was.
Your mother's face contorted then and the dagger look came
in her eyes that always presaged danger.

What Emma had left behind she plundered through. There were old shoes, odd stockings, an angora jersey, and some underwear. One stocking had a huge rosette of dried nail varnish on the thigh and the strap of a black brassiere was knotted and reknotted industriously. Nice milieus, nice milieus, your mother said and instanced the story about the swimming pool and the hot bouillon. Laid into the cups of the brassiere were two foam pads and when she held it up they tumbled out. She did not retrieve them, she would not allow you to, she was savage with Emma's belongings. Under the pillow was the sanitary towel, stained, but not blood-stained. Under the mattress Emma's diary. She flicked through it, pausing at nothing, expecting to light upon the clue, the confirmation.

She sent you for her glasses but as soon as she started to read she realized that the disclosures were sacrilege. She sat on the bed. She gasped, she said between those pages there was a cesspool, a veritable Hades, a chronicle of vice and filth. She asked her Maker why this cruel cross, she shook, she went into a paroxysm, she enumerated her life's woes, the skein of woes, she put two and two together, and asked whom she could turn to, in her hour of need.

He called from downstairs, asked in Moses' name where his dinner was. It was in the lower oven, drying up. She put the diary under the mattress and ran down, apologizing. He said why wasn't the table laid, why wasn't the pepper and salt and relish put down, he let out a tirade about the lateness of the hour.

You stayed behind. The thought of looking at the diary made you sick, made you squirm. You were both hot and cold. Your temples were hot and so were your eyeballs because of the way the blood rushed behind them but at your extremities you were cold.

You put two fingers in. You touched it. What were you doing? What were you doing? It was a sin. It was a sin against two Commandments. You took it out and opened it and your eyes raced from page to page, pouring over it, words, names, a rhyme:

Tony, thee I love
Long for thee I've tarried
Let's have jinks tonight
But no kids until we're married.

There were no appointments in it, nothing practical like that. It was all about men, what they did to her, what she did to them, how hot they were. Emma was fanatic with how hot they were. She called their yoke their apparatus. A school inspector had put Emma across his knee and thrashed her, hard. You had heard of him, he was famous, he was a famous native speaker. There were hurley players, a bus conductor, a policeman, a school inspector, a member of parliament, and an Italian who was a hat manufacturer. Emma had put the profession and the amount of money spent on her beside each one along with the details of what they did in private. The bus conductor spent nothing on her, had brought her to a park near the terminus late one night. Emma had a rendezvous with two men in the same evening, one at six, and the other, a medical student, at eleven in the night. After that she put *Living at last.*

You were boggled. You began to read them all over again. Your mother told you to come down at once. You went down sucking the corner of your handkerchief.

She had gone outside to pound potatoes. She worked the pounder around and around, used both hands and was prodigal with her strength. Steam completely blotted her face. The big potatoes she bruised by pressing them against the side of the saucepan. Hens perched on her bent back and were occupied trying to depose each other.

Ambie came and stood beside her and watched her pound potatoes that were already ground to a mash. The aluminum ring on his little finger flashed like mad as he raised it to scrape the tartar from his front teeth. He was biding his time. He said a little bird told him that a porker was on the way. She looked up, affronted. Her face was the color of porridge. He said Emma sent a wire to the doctor: Went over cliffs but still the same. Worried. He said the whole village was buzzing with it and not only that but farmers who might never have heard of it were discussing the substance, the wording, with each other. There was a pig fair on.

Your mother said Jesus Mary and Joseph like she had never said it before. Ambie told her the doctor had chosen to go on the batter and that a queue of people waited outside the dispensary either for him to return or to send that fop, the locum from the next village. He said the doctor had been called to Della at dawn and when he got there proceeded to examine her mother and later fell over the bed while looking into Della's tonsils.

Her eyes were dark and shiny as sloes. She asked how far gone he thought Emma was. She was frank with him. His own disgrace with the doctor's maid was forgiven, forgotten, in this new catastrophe. He said he thought five or six months. She thought less. They bickered over it. They discussed symptoms. She said Emma showed no lack of appetite, and referred to her own biliousness that was perpetual throughout her pregnancies. She hoped against hope. You were not told to go away. She said a diary upstairs contained the most lurid information conceivable. She said a checkered life went on in the metropolis away from home.

Ambie said Ah, stop. You could see that he was agog to look at the diary, to pour over it. He said a second communication had come, from a hospital, regarding a thing called a zondek. He recited it, Zondek positive. He said the bus conductor had brought in a bottle to the hospital and said it was either wine or urine.

She erupted. She said any fool would know it had to be urine, as what would a hospital want with wine, enjoined him to use his common sense on the matter. Emma had had to pass water into a bottle the night in the dispensary and maybe that was why he put the light out. Emma would have had to crouch over the bottle and funnel it in either with guesswork or the aid of a hand.

Ambie said it was on everyone's agenda and that he himself had incurred some of the obloquy. She said to stop being hypocritical and flounced off with a following of hens behind her.

Emma arrived by bus and hurried up the avenue. Your mother said she was to be given no refreshments but watched until such time as she could go to the doctor, until it fell dark. Emma made the mistake of humming as she entered the kitchen and she did a little wave of the hand by way of saying hello. He was out counting cattle.

She was radiant. The sulphur water had cleared her skin and there was not a pimple on it and not a blackhead. Her eyebrows were heavily penciled, in an unbecoming shade of brown. One line was crooked.

Your mother produced the diary, brandished it before Emma's eyes and said what was the meaning, what was the significance. Emma showed extreme presence of mind. She laughed and said Oh that. She said she was trying her hand at being a playwright, she said all for Hecuba, and that the play was the thing. She cited dramas that had thrilled her in her teens, East Lynne, Dracula, Murder in the Red Barn, and she also trotted out the names of the players who had been in them.

Your mother said a likely yarn and called her Madame. One of her real barbs. She pointed out that the diary was a tale neither of murder nor of love, but like an extract from the annals of a white slave trafficker.

Emma tried to snatch it from her, saying it was personal property but it got consigned to your mother's apron pocket and you watched its shape through the cloth, which was thin. You could not look Emma in the eye, you were too aghast.

Emma said there was no need to explode and was off on another tack about it being written at the behest of someone else, someone who was blackmailing her. Your mother shook her head and said Alas, alas, said a liar needed a great memory. Your mother was scrutinizing her from head to toe. Emma talked quickly and wildly, said it was true she had had an internal complaint that resulted in flatulence and that had mystified two specialists but that it had been properly diagnosed by her own doctor and had some cumbersome Latin name. She said there was no need for hysterics.

Your mother asked if she was bleeding. Emma prevaricated. Your mother took her by the shoulders and insisted upon being told. You dreaded what she might do. You were on Emma's side. Emma said she was spotting. They were both red in the face, Emma was a port wine color and your mother was beetroot like the Nigger. Emma flared up and said for pity's sake to postpone the dramatics until evening, until after she had seen her doctor and had the whole thing clarified. Such sudden authority shook your mother, made her hesitate, made her balk. Then Emma lost her footing, she put her hand out and each finger begged to be united with your mother's, to be interlocked. That resumed the hostilities, made her say that the writing was upon the wall. It was a bit like the song Mrs. Durack, as a bride, sang in the screechy voice, only it was not a bridle hanging on the wall, it was a catastrophe. Emma said there was nothing to be fatalistic about but the opposite was true. It was adjourned.

Emma begged to be let make pies to pass the time. Your mother went and picked rhubarb. The stalks were young and the skin came off in threads. When she chopped it a pink juice oozed from it which Emma tasted by dipping her finger in it from time to time. They worked together but without speaking. Emma put an inverted eggcup in the center of the heaped fruit and covered the whole thing with a very thin tent of pastry.

She said she went three evenings a week to a vocational school. She said there was nothing like bettering oneself. She addressed you but it was for your mother to register. Each time when you were on the point of saying something to Emma the words got caught in your throat and you could neither say them nor forget them and you could not utter them. You were like someone with a muzzle. Emma must have thought it was enmity, because she stuck her tongue out at you.

It was arranged that Ambie would go early to the doctor and pinion him down. It had to be after dark. Emma had to be ready to hide from your father. The news would have to be broken to him by imposing people, the doctor and Co. You were put looking out for him, you were the lookout person. There was no knowing from which direction he might come.

You ran from one side of the house to the other and sometimes you thought you saw his lank figure with the long nap
overcoat wide open and flapping at either side. But it was
only a figment you saw. You were banking on the dogs to
come first, to be his precursors the way St. John the Baptist
was the precursor of Christ. You thought that if only you
could go and forestall him and break it to him, that it would
be a coup for you and a blessing for Emma but that would
be the red rag to the Gaelic bull. You knew the altitudes of
his anger. Your limbs felt the onslaught of events.

She did not let Emma out of sight. When Emma went to
the pantry she followed and likewise when Emma went to
the front room to sit. She exclaimed when she spotted Lizzie
coming up the avenue with a cane, said did anyone ever see
such gall. She locked the door but did not put the big key in
its customary place on the narrow window ledge, she
brought it with her into the hall and up the stairs where you
followed. You tiptoed although Lizzie was quite a bit away
from the house. She tried the latch, then banged on the
door, then raised the window, then walked around the house
asking the hedge and devils pokers where everyone had van-
ished to, emphasizing that she hadn't seen a sinner go in or
out by the front gate. She tried the hall door as if she were a
visitor. She rapped first on the wood and then on the panes
of stained glass between the wood. She used a medal or
money because it was a metallic sound.

You were all crouched under the window and could hear
your hearts beating but you did not look at each other.
Theirs seemed in danger of bursting. You could also hear the
wind rushing between the strands of paling wire. The main
dilemma then was that Lizzie and your father might clash

and that it would be broken to him thus precipitately, disastrously.

Lizzie yelled up, and said Attention please. She had used her hand as a loudspeaker because her voice was both loud and more muffled. She said If she were mine I'd walk her through the town and hold my head high, and then there was a deathly silence while she must have been stepping over the grass and getting across the paling wire because there was no further announcement and you were on tenterhooks until she was far enough down the avenue to be sighted.

She moved like a harrier. Your mother remarked on it, on the caper of her. Your mother said Another candidate for the lunatic asylum and without too long an interval either. Emma concurred.

Your mother kept wondering aloud how your father ought to be told and then she went through the chain of events that was likely to ensue. It was amazing the things she could think of, the pinnacles of disaster to which her imagination rose. The weapons with which she supplied him, from the simplest thing like a slashhook to the most fearful like the bulldog revolver even though it was up in the river where she'd slung it, herself.

He blundered into it. The doctor, who was supposed to receive Emma in the dispensary, arrived instead at the hall door and was met by him returning with a lantern because he had gone to see to a sow who was with bonhams. The doctor shook his hand and said it was parlous, parlous, and how he would not have wished it on anyone, not even those mean demons who never paid his fees except in the form of poultry at Christmas time.

Your mother and you eavesdropped. The doctor was

drunk. He lit a cigarette so clumsily that it burst into sparks. She made a request for a cup of hemlock there and then and the same for you.

Your father thought it was about Giddy the mare that had to be shot and he said what grieved him altogether was that her flesh was sold in France as a delicacy and what savages the French must be. The doctor said he was speaking of Emma and asked pertinently if he thought the culprit, alias the prospective husband, was in danger of being a married man. He said the best they could hope for was a bachelor of means.

Your father got very sarcastic then and said Doc, I think you've had one over the limit. And the doctor biled at such a remark from a man he had so often treated for delirium tremens, got vituperative altogether and said Christ's sake man, open your eyes, she's five months gone. He added that it had been proven both by internal examination and with a urine test.

So it was urine. You elbowed your mother. She shook her fist at you to shut up. The hall door was shut but they could be heard clearly both because they were shouting and because two of the panes of stained glass were missing and the pieces of cardboard put in their place were missing too. She shielded the candle flame with her cupped hand. When they started to walk round the side of the house she hurried to be in the kitchen ahead of them and though she could have slain the doctor she bade him good evening in her customary diffident way.

But she was quaking. He put the lantern on the kitchen table with a thud. He was more gaunt than ever. There were two lights at the very time when a candle would have been excessive. The doctor kept blinking behind his glasses, was dazzled by the double assault on his eyes.

He tackled her. She was servile. She said she had been his wife, his obedient servant for upward of eighteen years. He said a nice thing, an obedient thing to hoodwink a man in his own house and did she think she'd go unharmed, because to disabuse herself of that. He said first and foremost to bring Emma out from under the bed so that he could gruel her and kick the guts out of her and give her the real Ally Daly of a beating.

She said for God's sake not to be like that, to let them club together and marshal their strength in their hour of need. He said he knew what he would marshal and took off his hat and began to go for her.

She said to have his will with her because she was already expiring and that it would be a mercy to finish her. The doctor intervened, said the situation was rife with anomalies. That made him gape.

The rhubarb pies had burned to a cinder and there was an atrocious smell. He said what a fine mess they were in, what a stew. The tea things were not cleared away. She begged him to sit, to restrain himself, to decide a plan of campaign.

She put three chairs close together for them to confer. He kicked one chair out of the way. Ambie let out two pronounced coughs to make known he was there in the event of combat. She had inveigled him to stay in and had installed him with three bottles of stout and a few hastily done ham sandwiches.

Your father opened the door intending to start the fracas but the moment he got the smell of the stout he proposed a drink. She gesticulated to say they had none. She was as versatile as the dummies. He said enough codswallop had gone on. He knew that the wines made from berries were bottles disguised under bits of cloth and stuck up the clefts in unused chimneys, fermenting, changing from fruit drink to wine drink, for the day when some visitor might call for hospitality. He said Shag it, she had her own jollop.

The doctor raised his hand and said firmly that if he had anything it would have to be spirits, some dry satin gin, because wine disagreed with his digestion. He meant of course her wine. For a minute the big dilemma was should they go to the pub or send the youngster for a bottle. She pleaded with the doctor not to go, not to leave.

You were torn in your wishes. It meant another expedition for you down the fields but at night now, with all the dangers that lurked. You insisted on walking. On a bicycle you could be surrounded, capsized, cornered, gripped, but not on foot because you were fleet of foot. Even your father admitted that. She stayed out of doors and every so often you said Yoo-hoo to make certain that she had not reneged. Her replies were faintness itself. You did not look to left or right into spheres of darkness and you did not look down either for cowpats or for stones though your feet had to contend with both. The small stones that your feet encountered made a steady racket as they rose and fell to a definite cacophony. You were hailed in the village. You were saluted by old men who had to ask other men aloud what your first name was.

The publican wrote the debt into the ledger and said it was a pleasure, his pleasure, and asked how your mother and father were and all their worldly goods and chattels. He asked if you wanted any trimmings with it, any mineral water or any *It. It* was what ladies added to their drinks to make them into cocktails, but knowing that neither your mother, Emma, or you would be imbibing, you said no and thanked him, but feebly.

There was no topic to compete with Emma's that night. The wireless was on but nobody was listening to it. The bottle was bulbous shaped. You held it to your breast, clasped it like a baby. He had put newspaper round it.

Your mother put a trickle in a glass, then drowned it with sugar and water. That was for him. She gave the doctor a huge measure. As soon as he tasted his he put the tumbler down and said to cut out the namby-pamby and walked to the pantry where she had put the remainder under a colander, alongside some cold cabbage. To spite her he put the bottle to his lips and said to the doctor to forgive the contamination but that a man in his position needed the patience of Job. He brought out the cold cabbage for the doctor to help himself to. It was green cabbage and some strips were darker than others and the stalk was soft and white.

He stamped on a newly lit cigarette. The doctor said Now, now, said that equilibrium was called for, and to bow to the slings and arrows of outrageous fortune. He winked at you when saying that. Your father began rolling up his sleeves. The doctor said they all had the same failing, hasty tempers and how it got them into scrapes all over the place and your father laughed recalling fistfights about such issues as the best goalie in the county or the maiden name of John McCormack's mother. Your father said that one thing he always made a point of was to stand a round of drinks after the furor had died down. The doctor said that was a good ruse, not to burn one's boats completely. Your mother ran her thumbnail against the grain of her lisle stocking and you pressed your hands to both ears to blot out the sound and there was buzzing in your head, but then you removed your hands so as to be alert for the arrival of Emma. You reckoned that she was outside the dispensary waiting, skulking in the doorway like a hen. The lantern gave a few puffs and then went out. Nobody bothered to wind down the screw. He said she was to make tea and toast.

Making toast involved opening the bottom door of the cooker, taking out a metal rack and holding the bread in close to the fire. She used the worst fork. She could have chosen a longer one, but she was bent on sacrifice. She buttered each slice as it was made and crushed the crusts with a knife to soften them. She gave it to them slice by slice in turn. She coughed a lot, dry conspicuous coughs with no phlegm in them.

There was something wrong with your swallow. It was like the day you ate the oyster, only you were choking from within yourself and the saliva kept threatening to engulf you. The doctor said the youth of the country had gone to hell, he cited his own son, called him a young lad instead of his name, which was Terence. She said Emma was always given too much latitude and too much longitude, by some. The doctor said that children were almost inevitably a disappointment, except for the infant muling and puking who provided some sort of puppy pleasure. She supplied a proverb: Sharper than a serpent's tooth is a thankless child. Then she looked at you and said Not you darling.

The darling was like an embrace in the big sorrowful kitchen. Your father said that he would have to marry her. She just nodded her head, she made no mention of the diary, no mention of the fact that there was a cavalcade of men, of suitors. The doctor said it was their blackest hour, their Via Dolorosa. She relished that.

Ambie appeared. He made sure not to look at her because of having bungled the night's arrangements. He had assured her that the doctor would be waiting to receive Emma in the dispensary. The doctor got it wrong being inebriated. Ambie kept eying the gin but was offered none. The level was sinking rapidly. Your father was insisting that when Emma showed up the doc must take her upstairs for a last thoroughgoing examination. Your mother was against that. The doc said they would decide anon. You were asked to leave.

You tiptoed out of the kitchen and through the hall. You crept into a downstairs room and nearly fainted, because there she was, there someone was, on a sofa, sobbing. You yelled. She cautioned you to shut up. They called in to know what ailed you and you said you had tripped on a biscuit tin, that was all.

She had climbed in the window. You closed the door. She was crying. It was more pitiful than any you had heard before. It was more like retching than crying.

You asked what was the matter. She said she could not bear to tell you. You asked three times, in the same tone of voice. Your voice was pinched, and your heart too, your heart was like a fist, clenched.

She said the doctor had just told her the sad news that she was barren and how it would jeopardize her chances of marriage. You did not know which to say first, whether to say he was in the kitchen, or to tell her that she was not barren, she was not like Sarah the wife of Abraham, or to ask if her husband-to-be was called Tony, short for Anthony. In the dark

you were only shapes to each other and it was a mercy that
you did not have to look her in the eye. You wanted to put
your arms around her but something stopped you, something in her repelled you. Her sins.

Her talk was scattered. She said she would shake them,
she would give your mother something to atone for. She said
like Caesar she could declaim Veni, vidi, vici. She said your
mother had warped and coddled you but then she took that
back and said that you were a mite and that she loved you almost. She said that in the spa town she and another had jit-
terbugged and had brought the crowd to a halt. She said she
was taking up fencing. She said the diary was nothing but a
pastime and that anyone who couldn't see that was very nar-
row-minded indeed. She expressed a desire for Bovril. She
said the dispensary was a dungeon. She said the doctor was
good at diagnosing but very abrupt and had told her about
being barren without as much as offering a handshake.

You tried to get a word in, you kept saying Please Emma,
and she said she wanted no sympathy, no commiseration,
she would brave it alone the way she had braved everything
and you said Please Emma and the door flew open and they
appeared with Ambie a few paces behind, holding the lamp.
He held it high and a little to one side to give himself a full
view.

Suddenly it was like a tribunal with them on one side and
Emma backing away in the direction of the fireplace. Her
feet were very far apart and the bow of her legs more pronounced than ever. She had had rickets when young, another thing which she held against her mother. She was like
the curlew, the grallatorial bird, in the lurch.

Your father went toward her to hit her but the doctor

pulled him back and said to keep in mind her condition, perfidious though it was. Your mother said she was a fully-fledged streetwalker. Your father asked what pack of lies she would like to unleash before he polished her off. She turned to the doctor and said could she have a word with him in private. Your father said all the private shit was over and that it was now in the public domain. A tick, she said, to straighten something out. He said no more shit, no more tautology.

He kept telling her to dry up, and at the same time plying her with questions, demanding a complete dossier on all her activities. Every time he approached her she took a few steps to the side to try and thwart him. He said ducking him was no good. He said it was her last moment under his roof.

She appealed to the doctor to side with her. He nearly succumbed but your father intervened and said what a traitor he was, what a turncoat. He called for an examination there and then, pointed to the couch. Your mother said to have some decency, some vestige of it. Emma went to your mother then but your mother said it was no use currying favor with her, no use at all.

From the way she shivered it was evident that she thought they were going to kill her. Her movements were beyond her governing, legs, knees, teeth, everything, chattered. The doctor said Steady now, and tried to improve his focus by taking off his glasses, and rubbing both of his eyeballs roughly and putting his glasses back on again. Your father asked if it could be prevented. The doctor said that was a moot point. Your father said wasn't there ergot. Your mother uttered an ejaculation, a grandiloquent one, recalled the incident of the doctor's maid and the nine layers of blood-soaked newspaper. Ambie got shifty, went to the window and looked out at the dark night and started to whistle. Your father said he wanted something done and pronto at that. The doctor said indeed. Your father said it was a little matter of circumventing nature. The doctor said there was such a thing as professional ethics. Your father said to ethic his arse and play ball and do something. The doctor said to cut out the follols and put it in plain speaking, and was it to terminate a life he was being asked, was that the gist. Your mother said In the name of God. Your father said everyone was putting the wrong construction on his idea. Your mother said But. Your father said to but him no buts. The doctor said to remember the Fifth Commandment, Thou Shalt Not Kill. Your father went back on it then, said his head was addled, said everyone was against him, conspiring.

Emma clutched her stomach. It was hard to think that something else breathed inside her. You couldn't accept it. It needed a squeal or a pram to convince you of a baby. Her death would have simplified everything then. It was the only solution. It was what you all wanted, her death and her burial. Ambie sighed and put the lamp on the table with faulty castors and as your mother ran to rescue it Emma fell in a heap on the floor. The grueling was too much for her.

The two emergencies took everyone by surprise. The doctor went to her, picked her arm up, felt her pulse, winked, said she would be better before she was twice married. Your mother made no secret of the fact that she found his remark in extreme bad taste. Emma refused to say anything.

She looked scandalous. The hooks and eyes of her skirt wide open. You invented penances for her, for her face to be covered in sweat, her hair streaming, her walking on a bed of nails, going toward an altar with an agnus dei, a lamb of God, prostrating herself, getting cleansed, getting forgiven, eventually getting canonized. The doctor said a bit of sedation was called for and your father said strychnine would be better and he stressed the dosage in case anyone thought he was feigning it.

You had a heartburn. The yolk of an egg burned in your gullet. Your mother told her to get up and compose herself. Lying with her legs apart it was as if she was waiting to be sacrificed there and then. The doctor began to be practical. He told her they would have to find the gent in question and have banns read and arrange for wedding bells. Poor Emma he said, in the lexicon of youth, poor Emma. Your father told her to speak up, to give the man's name, occupation, earnings, and character. Your mother said not to use the word character in that context. Your father told your mother to keep out of it, that it was business between men and he and the doctor hefted Emma onto the leather pouffe. She swayed. They got from her a name and a working address for the man she held responsible. She didn't know his home address. Idiotically she told them that he was one of a family of seven.

Your mother, who knew the disclosures in the diary, took no interest in the plot that was being hatched to find this man and get him to the altar. She started tidying, she straightened the antimacassars and thumped the cushions. She said Emma might as well go to bed.

Emma rose and headed for the door. Your father said did she want grub. She said no. He said to do as she was told. Your mother said to let her off. He said he wanted none of her invective and to go and polish his good shoes because he and the doc had a call to make, to thrash things out, to decide on protocol, to get the bugger to the altar without any snags. She went behind his back and beckoned to the doctor not to encourage him in that escapade. In the shoe closet mice had congregated. There was a smell of leather and the perspiration from the insides of shoes.

He exclaimed when he saw the mice, asked for the salt-cellar, said

There's going to be a race,
Five asses and a ginnet
And I bet you two to one
That the Father's ass will win it.

He said mice could be stopped in their tracks, mystified, by putting salt on their tails and he tried it and when it didn't paralyze them he flung shoes, a last, every conceivable object. The doctor and he took bets as to who would make the first slaughter. They were exhilarated by it. The mice went clambering up the walls in desperate attempts to escape the various peltings. The saltcellar got emptied. A dying mouse let out a last and unbecoming screech and he asked your mother to loan him a tanner so that he could honor his debt. He was livid at having lost.

In the morning she put on her good corset which meant she was making a journey. He shaved on the kitchen table and she put saucers as protection over the milk, the butter and the sugar. He held his face sideways and drew the razor quickly over his jaw. In disposing of the lather he managed to strew blobs everywhere except in the small china bowl that she had given him for the purpose. She was fearless, taxed him with his crudeness of the night before, said he had

shown his true colors. He looked at her with the razor poised
in her direction, and though all of her was immobile, her
Adam's apple kept jumping up and down. When she did not
cower he laughed and asked if she'd got out the wrong side
of the bed. He said there was no fooling him and that to
admit it that she was thrilled at the excuse of having a day
out, a day in the metropolis.

When Emma appeared he was the one to suggest that she
eat something and she was the one who quickly and pointedly removed the jam in order to deprive Emma of a delicacy. Alone at the far end of the table Emma chewed bread
distractedly. You had this silly thought that if you met him
you might fall in love with Emma's intended and she and
you would be contending for him. Your mother mixed various foodstuffs for you to give to the hens throughout the
day. You wished that you could go.

He was civil to Emma. He asked was it so that the manager of a big hotel had lost his only son in a bus accident.
Emma said yes. He said he heard that it was like a battlefield,
all the dead bodies, all the carnage and Emma said being a
busload it probably was.

You kept passing bread to her and when they were leaving
you kissed her goodbye, anxious to give her that sign, that
little token of loyalty. You tidied. You read a poem called The
Hound of Heaven, how the hound of Heaven pursued a
soul. You could picture the hound running round and
round, tracking this soul, this Emma, fleeing it down the
nights and down the days and down the arches of the years.
The doctor had termed it copulation, you would look up
that word in the dictionary, in the school dictionary, one
day, in time to come. The doctor's maid had told someone

that once a woman got a taste for it she could never give it up, it got to be a craving, like a craving for sweet things or cigarettes. You could picture them calling at the office of Emma's intended, his being told to go out in the corridor to receive a deputation. You felt for him even though you didn't know him, hadn't even seen a photo of him. You tried standing on one foot, without wobbling, so that everything would be all right. If you could do it for sixty seconds it meant he would marry her. Standing on your right foot was easier than standing on your left, the opposite would have been the case if you had been left-handed. You were not left-handed but you were double-jointed. There would be a wedding, but not a white wedding. You might be bridesmaid. His parents and your parents would meet.

Ambie said it was gas, all this blood and thunder but that in spite of it decent people had to eat. He was pushing cabbage into bacon water. The level of the water rose up over the edge of the saucepan and when it fell onto the hotplate the water made a terrible racket and ran into little beads. He said he could eat a young child.

Your father would have taken umbrage at such innuendo. You said you were fasting for a special intention. He said what intention. You pretended it was an examination and talked a bit about your studies. You said needlework and singing were your worst subjects. He said he had socks to be darned and would you like a bit of practice. You said it was buttonholes you were bad at. He said he could do with buttonholes too, and buttons. He pointed to the numerous safety pins on his person. His trousers were held up with a canvas belt that he had knotted. Above it was a bulge of fat, pinkish.

For a minute you were afraid, afraid that he might copulate with you. He dropped the sweater over the belt and over the assembly of safety pins. The end of the sweater was raveled and for fun he took hold of one of the loose threads, pulled it and raveled it more. He said he would teach you how to sing. You both sang If I were a Blackbird, and now and then when it was going nicely he stopped and let you sing alone but the moment you realized you were unaccompanied you stopped too and put your hand to your mouth in embarrassment. Then you both began again.

He said you definitely had an ear and a melodious voice and that with a small amount of practice you could do nice renderings and go on stage and get bouquets, and eventually marry a boxer or someone lusty like that. You said he could be a boxer if he trained. You enumerated his skills, his green fingers, his pig killing, his cunning with the cards.

The cabbage was boiling but the water had stopped boiling over and the smell made your mouth water. It had lost its crinkle and each strip was like a ribbon. He put a bit on the end of a fork and brought it to your lips to see if it was tender enough. It was. He said Emma would be eligible for oranges and wasn't it a most contradictory state of affairs. He laid places for two. You agreed to eat but you knew you were letting Emma down and because you had promised to fast that it was a similar bargain as between God and Moses in the desert, and that as long as Moses kept his arms aloft the tribe won but the minute he lowered his arms the tribe lost. For every mouthful you ate, Emma was being put through some worse ordeal. You did not rule out miscarriage. You also thought of quins. There were quins in the world and your heart rent for their mothers and all the stitchings their mothers would have after such emissions.

Ambie put mustard and brown sugar on the bacon fat. It was sweet and juicy. He told you not to split on him but that he had an offer of a job in England in a factory. He told you that his brother was there and what he earned and how much he liked it, and how he wasn't completely cut off from nature because he also had an allotment of thirty rods where he grew potatoes and lettuce. He said how his brother's wife belonged to a club which allowed her to save money every week so that she had a haul at Christmas with which to buy hampers and things.

It seemed a perfect life. He said his brother's wife had a job, stringing pearls in her own home and earning pin money for herself. Ambie said that when he first got to England he would stay with his brother but that later on he would have a place of his own. He did not specify a wife but you knew that somewhere in his expectations there figured a woman who would string pearls and at the same time be at home rearing children and cooking the dinner.

He was so emboldened by it that for a moment you forgot Emma, but then it came back like a pain after a lull. Through the window you could see the dogs. They looked in at you. They were waiting for their dinner. Automatically you started to scoop the potatoes out of their skins and mash them. You made pandy for the dogs. You used his plate and yours. He took milk from the jug. He could drink a great slug without stopping. When you opened the door and called them the dogs bounced in and they were so pleased they nearly spoke to you. He asked in Christ's name how you were ever going to get them out again. You said it did not matter.

They appeared like two figures in a painting, dark brown figures, trundling along, on some sort of pilgrimage. At least he was sober, he was not staggering. You ran to meet them and your mother said it was too chilly for you to be out without a coat. She had no packages, no presents. You told her that you got nineteen eggs.

First thing she did before taking off her coat was to put the kettle on. They had not broken their fast since morning. You proffered the cold bacon but your father said he could only eat bread and milk. She crumbled white bread into a saucepan of milk and put it to boil slowly and stirred it so that it was smooth. While she was doing that she ate a piece of bacon from her fingers and remarked that it was delicious. He said not to tantalize him by telling him that something he couldn't have was delicious. He was briary, found fault with everything, went to great lengths to kick the dogs. He had had a haircut. The tops of his ears showed. The tops of his ears looked narked. They must have had time to spare. You said what a nice haircut it was. He didn't answer. Where had they left Emma? What was happening? When was the wedding? When would you know?

They ate in silence. Afterwards, she said the least they could do was go and tell the doctor, tell him the developments. He said he had no intention of going anywhere.

She and you went. Her good coat was on the chair where she had put it down when she came in, her gloves in the pocket. She debated whether or not she should change her shoes, then didn't. He had his head lowered onto his hand and with the other hand was scratching his scalp abstractedly. There were no goodnights.

She spelled things for the doctor, she spelled the words rather than say them. She said it was all U-P. She talked with the doctor outside his house where she had waited to catch him, not being on speaking terms with his wife. She sent you off to have a little walk, a little constitutional.

You stood a decent distance away and there were things you heard and things you didn't. The doctor said yes-yes to everything she said. The two yeses were significant. He was not nearly as expansive as the previous night.

She said the gentleman in question was nothing but a gurrier. She went into details over his garb and his accent. He wore a blazer with brass buttons and his trousers were gray flannel. He was the sporting type. His accent she said had to be heard to be believed, likewise his impertinence. She called him a pup. Then she said gurrier. Then she reverted to pup. She said he had the audacity to light a cigarette, remained as cool as a breeze.

The doctor pressed her to summarize. He wanted the net

result. She said the net result was that he had turned to Emma and said What about the others, the Tom, Dick, and Harrys. She said to top everything Emma had the audacity to sob.

The doctor said was he or was he not marrying her. She said that not only was there no marriage but that he suggested Emma toss for it to know which of the men on the team was the donor. They had put Emma in lodgings with some devout lady, some good Samaritan who took care of such people.

She did not say so but it was evident that they had located this lady through a friend of theirs, Father Scanlon, who had a parish in the city. She kept saying that only for the priest they would have been sunk. The baby itself was eclipsed in all the talk about the priest and the devout lady and the pup with the blazer.

Then she addressed the doctor by his first name, a daring thing for her, who was on first name terms with no one except her sister, your Aunt Bride; and she pleaded with him for an honest answer and she said could it be some disease Emma had, something hereditary, from her father's side of the family, perhaps. He said it was a moot point and he did not think so.

They were silent for a minute, she sighing and he going through his bunch of keys to find the one to his hall door. It was time to go. He kissed her once, then twice, and they were noiseless kisses and she stayed in his arms for a second, content. You knew about them being attached, from the day on the kitchen table but you knew too how assiduously they denied themselves each other's company. He said to be of good heart, to be of good cheer, to be invincible. Quickly he went in home. Only then did she break down.

You took her hand. You were very familiar with it. Her hand in yours was weightless.

When anyone saluted she did not answer, she did not want to be greeted. The lights in most of the houses were gone out and twice she turned on her ankle. Passing Della's house there were lights in each of the four small windows and it was like Christmas Eve but you knew in your bones that Della had died then, although you did not know it officially until Ambie brought word from the creamery the following morning.

When you went to the wake she was lying on her back and all the color had been drained from her cheeks and her cheeks were as white as her hands. She was wearing a brown habit with scapulars to match. She was too young for brown but that was the color the undertaker stocked. The film stars were covered over with a bit of white sheet. Nearly everything was white, the candles, the counterpane drawn up and folded under her chin, the two flowers in a vase. They were plastic lilies.

She was holding a crucifix in her hand, holding it tight, like she was clenching it. You thought it funny that her will should be dead but her grasp alive, and you wondered if her soul had got there, if it had been told of its abode for all eternity. It took some time for the soul to make the journey and no one knew exactly how long it took. She had been dead for nearly twenty-four hours.

Her mother sobbed away steadily and though she moved her lips nothing in the way of speech came out. Each time the door opened the candle sputtered. The floor was newly varnished and those with heavy steps stuck to it. When they lifted their shoes it was an effort and they made a squelching sound.

After an appropriate amount of prayer you went downstairs for refreshments. You sat between your mother and father. Everyone was eying them, waiting for them to divulge, to say something about Emma. Your father refused a clay pipe. The clay pipes had a funny smell and they made a hollow sound when the men tapped them on the table. You were afraid your teacher might come in and make an example of you. You had missed school three days in a row. You wanted never to have to go back to school. You prayed that you might get consumption, or scarlet fever, or to inherit a legacy and employ a tutor. There would be nudging about Emma. No girl would link you or have a stroll with you at playtime. You would be ostracized.

Lizzie appeared from the kitchen. She had broken the pledge. She towered over your mother and asked if it was permitted to partake of the same oxygen. Your mother said certainly but her voice was strained. You went as red as anything. Lizzie said that some people, hitherto friends, had the gall to bar doors and windows in her face. Ambie tried to intervene because he hated to see women sparring but Lizzie just pushed him away with her elbow. She said it was all right to call on Lizzie, to incommode her when a loaf of bread, a jar of nutgall ointment, or a quid was needed but it was all wrong if she offered a helping hand about a more grievous matter.

Your father was bristling. You could just foresee him hitting her and her skull cap falling off and it being very awkward and disgraceful. Fortunately a miracle occurred.

A frog jumped out of the ashes and everyone started screaming and yelling and all deference for the corpse was forgotten as the room became a hubbub of noise and pandemonium. Your father took the initiative. He took the tongs and felt in the fire to see if there were any others. He said there might be a litter. Two other men were trying to chase it out. The door was held open. It was a rabid dark outside. A stray dog rushed in to add to the consternation.

It was a black dog and people kept warning each other not to move, not to do anything to it, to keep still. A black dog and the devil were one and the same. The frog darted back to the middle of the floor and then the dog started chasing it around and around in a circle and men were shouting at each other to kill it, to kill them both. Your father asked was there a shotgun. You distinctly heard your mother say Oh Jesus, oh no.

The frog was in a tizzy and was trying to escape at all costs, using any outlet, getting under chairs and advancing in any direction, but always the dog was on its track either with its paw or with its tail or with its nose. It was a hunting dog without doubt. Someone said it was a cur and no earthly cur at that. There was a sudden squelch as the frog's intestines spewed all over the floor after one of the men had succeeded in trampling on it. Unaccountably the dog departed.

Della's mother, who had come down to see what all the ructions were about, was led back up the stairs. It augured bad. The frog and its remains were shoveled and thrown in the fire and soon there followed a burned flesh smell. No one knew what to say.

People huddled closer to the fire, glad of its warmth but revolted by its smell. A woman said she had it on good authority that Hitler was anti-Christ. Someone else said that Hitler had a girl friend called Eva Braun. There was talk of a man who had died in France, fighting with the British. There was a bit of bitterness about that, some saying that to fight for the British was a scandalous thing. The women said wasn't it terrible for his mother and how she didn't know he was dead and how she watched for the mail to come every day expecting news of him, and even went to the post office while the letters were being sorted out. His mother was doting.

The person who held the floor was a girl home from England talking about the air raids. She described how one minute she was in the room of a house and how the next minute and after a rumble, the walls were gone and she was able to reach out and touch the branches of a tree that had fallen from the pavement. She was the only living thing in that household not to have got killed. The cats, the kittens, the mistress, the Austrian cook, everyone had got killed but her. She was a private nurse.

People said it was because she was a Catholic she had been so mercifully spared. Then someone said she heard that air-raid shelters were dens of vice and the Nigger said if it weren't for the fact that he hated pavements he would have been in the city long ago, but in Paris where the Follies of Bergère and the boulevards were. He did a swagger to show how he would acquit himself there. The wild geese had gone there, wild geese rising on clamorous wing, went to follow the night of an alien king.

There was a man sitting opposite you and he had half an ear and your mother leaned over to Lizzie who was sitting two places away and said I wonder what bit the ear off him, was it the devil, and they looked at each other and first did nothing and then they relented and your mother smiled a small smile, and Lizzie's face dissolved into a beam and they shook hands. Lizzie changed places so as to be next to your mother and they began to talk in a whisper and you knew that your mother was confiding.

On the way home your mother said there would be no happiness and no redemption, and Lizzie said there would, there would, to always remember the cross and the blood gushing from Christ's side, redeeming everything and everyone. They each swore to pray and make sacrifices and the Nigger who caught up with them said that maybe it was a bit of the male relic the ladies wanted, and then he panted and your mother pulled you near her and said to Lizzie that if the Nigger did any bestial thing to shout for help. Your father was some bit behind arranging with some man about getting the loan of a machine to mow his hay. Your mother and Lizzie and you formed a tight huddle and when the Nigger couldn't get any hearing he walked on and your mother said Once a ram always a ram and Lizzie said Ssh and not to exasperate him any further.

Going up the field your father predicted it would rain. The horses were standing under trees, in pairs. The cows were in a herd, wheezing and lying down. The moon was the shape of a sickle. It was a young moon. The Nigger said that the infinite bodies of the heavens affected all earthly things and that a person had only to look at the sea to apprehend how the full moon disturbed it. Butting from one horse was his stump, and it was stout and black and given to spasms and they were so regular you could have bet on their occurrence. You shut your eyes. Your mother said she hoped it would rain because happy was the corpse that the rain fell on.

In the cut hay there were flowers, meadowsweet and buttercups that hadn't yet died and hadn't yet withered. The hay was green. They cut it too soon because the man with the machine came and they had no choice. It would sweat and have a sour taste but the cows and the horses would munch it, and relish it, nevertheless. They were not fussy.

You lay on the ground. Your nose got tickled. The world was empty. The world was deserted. You didn't hear a dog or you didn't hear a bell, you heard nothing only your heart hammering. You contrived the rolls, so that you went from one green swarth to the next, skipping the grass in between, getting wet, getting intoxicated.

The only thing that might have alarmed you, that might have terrified you, was a frog or a field mouse. Nothing did. There were no snakes. St. Patrick had banished all the snakes. The snakes had gone to Australia, so had the convicts, so had the man that shot the girl because she refused him a drink, the man that shot and missed.

The sun looked to be near. The sun was gold. The moon was silver. Silver and gold you had none. Gold was being dug for in the mountains, and on the isle of Capri a man beheld a woman with a plain golden ring on her finger. Al Jolson had two wives, and still sang to his Mammy, sang Mammy, Mammy. The songs exploded in your head.

The sun and your heartbeat were far apart, the sun was a great gold fleshy orb, and your heart was a pump attending to its own bloodstream. You dreaded your bloodstream. You dreaded the red corpuscles more than the white because they were red, but you needed both to function.

You were mourning over Ambie. Went home on his biannual outing, then wrote to say he wasn't coming back. He had not written a letter before, hence the punctuation, which was calamitous. Your father said he was a bloody blackguard, said he wouldn't be surprised if he hadn't gone to be a hangman somewhere, because of his expertise with the knife.

You loved him. You had played love, like, hate, adore, and marry with his name and yours. According to it he and you would marry. You said it was because he couldn't bear partings, couldn't have suffered the goodbye, that made him sneak away. Your mother professed to never having cared for his folks, whom she had not met. Your aunt said that maybe he had found a sweetheart.

You sent him a letter in secret. You wrote Remembrance is all I ask, but if remembrance should prove a task, Forget me. It seemed a bit extreme once you had posted it.

The room was fourteen feet by nine. The wallpaper, a rustic pattern, had been put on upside down. Emma had had plenty of opportunity to take stock. Emma was huge.

She wore a black dress appliquéd with roses. You followed the protrusion of her stomach by following the circuit of the roses. Conversation was stilted. You did not look up.

Her hands were white, dead white like hands that had been immersed in water for a long time. The room was one hundred and seventeen square feet in area, you had worked it out. She said the visits from the priest were her one and only solace. She regretted the fact that she could not go out in the street because she would have liked to have seen what the autumn fashions were like. It was impossible for her to go out for fear she might bump into her boss or any of her friends. She said she felt very cooped up.

The lady who took care of her brought a tray with tea and arrowroot biscuits. Your father asked if he could have a slice of bread instead of an arrowroot biscuit. Your mother glared.

The landlady said no trouble at all. He said anything, even a crust would do. The landlady removed the two biscuits which would have been his and when she went out he said he believed in being outspoken. Your mother said there was a thing called outspokenness and there was a thing called politeness and they were two very different matters altogether. He said fancy that, annoying her even more by refusing to be riled.

When the landlady came back she said she realized what it was that you reminded her of. She laughed and said a horse.

They all looked at you. She said your neck. They looked at your neck but did not know what to say.

She left the bread on a small plate before him. He examined it before tasting it. It was a bit gray. Emma said the food was not at all appetizing. Your mother gave her a look and said they did not want to hear any complaints, that the strain on their funds was catastrophic. Emma said only for the lending library she would have gassed herself. Your mother said to retract that remark. Your father told your mother that it was not fair to upset Emma in her condition, and Emma began to cry but not expansively as of old. They were slow, bitter tears that she wrenched from herself.

Your mother produced the presents and handed them over in silence. The two packages were held together with a piece of rough string. In one box there was a cake and the cling peaches and in the other a pleated skirt for when Emma would be shapely again. It was plaid. Your mother had brought no baby clothes because it was already arranged that Emma's baby would be handed over to the State a few seconds after it was born.

Emma said she hoped it would be soon. He said to send

them a communiqué, a telegram. Your mother asked was it out of his mind he had gone, did he want the whole parish to know. He told her to be quiet. He said he had a brainwave. He said to Emma couldn't they use Morse code. Emma said they could if they knew Morse code but they didn't. He said surely there was some way of conveying secret information, the way the Germans did from the submarines.

Your mother said to stop talking rot. He hit the palm of his hand with his fist, said he had it. He said to Emma Now suppose it's a boy, we'll call that a Volkswagen; and suppose it's a girl, we'll call that a Hillman Minx. Then overjoyed with himself he worded the telegram, Arrived safely in Volkswagen or Arrived safely in Hillman Minx. He and Emma repeated it like it was a couplet. He slipped some money into the neckline of her dress. He was transported by the code. He wanted to tell it. He kept remarking over and over again of the seconds prior to his discovery and how he knew it was going to hit him, the solution.

You said it was a bit like Archimedes in his bath jumping up and down shouting Eureka when he found out about floating. No one of you could float. Your father said wasn't it remarkable how it took a catastrophe to bring out the brilliance that was in him. You said sweet were the uses of adversity.

Your mother looked at you and said enough nonsense had been aired and asked if he'd given Emma money because if so he had a screw loose. Having to pay for Emma's lodgings every week had completely banjaxed his finances. He said not likely but it was clear that he had.

When you thought of her protrusion your blood curdled and all of you hurt like you were being scraped throughout with a razor. You stretched your limbs but that made it worse. Your mother said why were you stretching like a hussy and to remember that you were in a train, a public vehicle, and not on a hammock, lounging. To your knowledge you had never lounged on a hammock.

You were the only people in the carriage. They had spread themselves out, put his hat and coat on two other seats to make it seem that they were reserved. She wanted to be private. She insisted on being private to discuss the visit, to keep emphasizing the wastefulness of it all.

You were consumed with the nightmare of Emma's belly. You thought you saw it move. You couldn't be sure but that it was one of her muscles or if there had been any movement at all other than a phantom one in your mind.

In the train lavatory everything got blurred. Black rings started to appear. They twinkled black. They moved into your brain, whole batches of them. Once they got in there they started swimming and merging together. They made a whirring noise like the spokes of a bicycle. They occupied your whole head. They were colliding. You fainted, but without anyone knowing. Not even you yourself knew.

You came to, holding on to the pedestal of a washbasin. You sucked your cheeks to get the color back. You splashed your face. The washbasin was font-shaped and chapped. A hen could have rested nicely in it.

The telegram said DIFFICULTIES WITH VOLKSWA-
GEN and they were demented at trying to interpret it, trying
to decide who was endangered, it or Emma. They argued
hotly as to whether Volkswagen stood for a boy or a girl, got
vituperative, he claiming one thing, she another. She said he
never listened, he was too headstrong. You were called in to
arbitrate.

You stood there wringing a bit of your skirt. It was clumsy
material and did not yield easily to your grasp. It was a rem-
nant, bought at the woolen mills after a fire had occurred.
She thought you were hesitating because of not daring to
take sides and she told you to go ahead, that nobody would
penalize you.

But you didn't know. At the time you had been smarting
under the fact that the landlady had likened you to a horse.
You shook your head.

He said a fine asset you were to any family or to any serious enterprise, with your scatter head and your scatter brain.

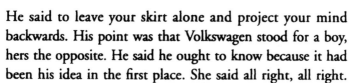

He said to leave your skirt alone and project your mind backwards. His point was that Volkswagen stood for a boy, hers the opposite. He said he ought to know because it had been his idea in the first place. She said all right, all right. That flummoxed him.

She said they would send a further telegram asking for additional information. It was dire getting the address of the maternity hospital, because the doctor, the only one they could ask, was in court that day, acting as a defense witness in a cottage murder case, but since his client was convicted they were late home, they were delayed, drowning their sorrows. A victory would have detained them too. Lizzie got it from the postmistress, and she had a cousin in labor, went into eulogies about her cousin's bone structure. She was purring when she handed it to your mother. The doctor was boggled by the telegram both because he was drunk and because the code had never been conveyed to him.

The one they sent back was peremptory. It said RE-QUIRE FULL DETAILS CONCERNING VOLKSWAGEN AND DRIVER IMMEDIATELY. It cost the most of ten shillings. Your father said to keep the change.

You cycled back and bought iced biscuits. The vans had arrived that day and there was a small flush of dainties in the shops. You had them with tea. The thin icing melted from the steam of the tea. You passed them around and he took three and the doctor took three and you were left with four.

At school girls looked at you and nudged each other. You were an aunt now. You thought it a disgraceful thing to be. The teacher made a point of being nice to you, got you to do errands, got you to light the fire which was her way of being nice.

The wet turf was a gift from your father to the school, a

whole kreel of it sent one day in the Emma era in a burst of righteousness, because tongues were wagging. Ambie had brought it. The big girls had to carry it in. Some were industrious and carried a whole armful but some just brought a sod in either hand so as to have the excuse to go back and be saucy with Ambie.

Still no word. They were on edge. It occurred to you that Emma might be dead. You pictured a wake with the women weeping and the dressmaker enumerating Emma's good points. You went so far as to have a baby laid out beside her in a matching habit and you supplied each of the corpses with a narcissus. It was a bit comical. He said what was the joke. You said nothing, no joke.

You practiced holding a baby by holding a big doll. The doll said ma-ma when you pressed her stomach. The place to press was hard and circular, was like a penny. You were an aunt. You all sat in the kitchen waiting. The fire you could not see. It was hidden behind porcelain and behind that again were layers and layers of asbestos. The asbestos was wound around and around like a person's intestine.

She hadn't lit a fire in the room in case you would all be called away suddenly. They snapped at each other for the least little thing. The kettle was the only contented sound, the kettle simmering away. She turned the spout inwards in case anyone should get burned. Each time he used it to make tea he put the spout facing outwards again. He made tea in a cup, enough for himself. He strained it from one cup to another and in the transaction spilled some of it. He let out various moans, pleas, prayers, a medley of curses. You could not hear the knobs of coal falling away or changing their properties inside the fire and yet you knew that it was hap-

pening and that there would be ashes to be emptied in the
morning. You wanted it to be morning. The prognostica-
tions were worse at night.

When she lifted the top to fuel it there was a shudder and
a dark blue flame bolted up. A horrible smell accompanied
that flame. Fumes got down the back of your throat and
made each of you cough. You each coughed differently. Your
coughs were your signature tunes. When she put the lid back
the smell still prevailed. She said they would be wanting fuel
soon.

The fuel had to be sent for, a long way off, to where it was
mined. There was no telling about each load. Sometimes
they got swindled, they got a load of slack but at other times
they were bright cones all fashioned to the same size and she
was as grateful as if she had won the sweep.

She kept going to the front room to look for the telegram
boy. He was easy to spot at night, being made conspicuous
because of the glow of his flashlamp. He was a dwarf. His
mother rarely let him deliver at night, claimed it was bad for
his chest.

Your father said any sign. She said if there had been any
sign she would have said so, proclaimed it from the rooftops,
said hosannah. It was one of the few times when she con-
tended. You wanted to applaud. You applauded in your
mind.

He said there was no need to bite the head off him, he had
only asked a civil question. She said it was inappropriate and
went again to the front room to look. He read the paper,
read births, marriages, and deaths, aloud.

By the following morning and after a sleepless night they
had the wind up. He said he'd better go and find Emma, and

bring her back. Your mother said no, she'd go, said it was a mother's place. Then she said you could go with her and the gym frock that you had put on for school you quickly unbuttoned on both shoulders and let slide to the floor. She fished out a brassiere for you, one that Hilda had given her. It was like being promoted, you were promoted to a brassiere.

The cups were too deep. She said to wear it outside your vest and you did, though that completely nullified its use. Your diddies were hardly formed. You got stinging pains in them from time to time. You discussed those pains with no one. You couldn't touch your diddies, not even with your own finger, and you couldn't touch the nipples either. The nipples were like warts only they were pink in color, whereas warts were flesh-colored and later brown when they withered away after caustic pencil had been applied to them. Hers were big and floppidy. They were agile.

You did not look at her directly but you saw the details of her person out of the corner of your eye. She tied her brassiere wrongly. A hook dug into her skin. She proposed to leave it so. Then she changed her mind, said it would persecute her for the whole day and hurriedly she took off her jumper and got you to appoint hooks and eyes correctly.

There were spare rolls of skin on her back. It was like blancmange, cold and white and appetizing. You didn't touch her.

In one respect she was glad to be going. She said she would get a lipstick. For years she had been hankering for a new one. Her old one was dry and was a color that in the cold emphasized the mauve pigment in her cheeks. Everyone had different tints, she had mauve on her cheeks and sallow on her neck and blancmange down the length of her back.

She carried the six bottles of cloudy wine to the turf house and buried them under turf mold so that there would be no danger of his finding them. She asked him not to break out. She made him vow. He kissed her, then he kissed you.

You had a way of ignoring his kiss, you let his mouth implant itself on you but you told yourself that you were not experiencing anything and in that way you didn't. You were like a statue except that you exuded fear. Animals could smell that fear. That was why they were not your friends.

He and the dogs saw you off. You put the big stone to the gate and stood to wait for the lorry. A lorry went to the city each week with lime because there was demand for it among the market gardeners.

Your mother had to borrow money from Lizzie. Lizzie waited with you at her gate and while she was waiting she kept pulling weeds and bits of grass from between the stones and from the congested flowerbeds. Her cat went across the road and she called after it Sib, Sib, Sib, and went and picked it up and brought it back. She intended getting a leash for it. She mentioned a film that was on in the city about mining in a Welsh valley. Your mother said there would be no time for diversions like that, or no money. Lizzie ran into the house and got another pound note which your mother made a to-do about accepting.

The seats of the lorry were very high and the leather ripped. You sat in the middle half on air, half on a seat. You resolved that if you had to let off a crack you would do so discreetly by making the cheeks of your bottom cleave together to muffle the sound. You rehearsed it. But of course you could not be sure that it would go noiselessly according to plan. The windows had to be kept closed to keep the lime from blowing in your eyes.

She was very polite to the driver, who was German, asked him how he thought the war was going. He had come years before to work on the installation of an electricity plant and had built a house and not gone home. Every time he touched the gear lever you shot over to your mother's side for safety. He had a reputation for clicking with ladies. He and the tailor were friends, went in late to Mass, together.

Your mother had to shout to be heard. They didn't say much. He got out on a stretch of road where there were no houses and no tillage and you made the mistake of asking why. Your mother nudged you but it was too late. He said pay-pay, getting the word for pee-pee wrong.

It was a bleak, brown vista, all bog. You knew you were in the center of the country, the flat basin that you had learned about at school, but had visualized differently. There were no crops and no pasture and no telling where it ended.

As you got to the outskirts of the city your heart began to race. The buildings were low and straggling, they were not like New York but you were delighted by them all the same. The chimney pots looked like series of tiny men standing to attention. Only then did she plot an itinerary.

She asked the German to drop her in the main street near a pillar. It was the only landmark she knew of. It was where country people made rendezvous. There was a statue at the top, representing an English general that people scoffed at or were belligerent about. You craned your neck but couldn't see him, couldn't have described him to anyone. The stone was sooted.

You went first to the house of the woman who said you

were like a horse. She was haughty. Then she lashed out, said not only had Emma skedaddled before the event but had left two weeks lodgings outstanding. She said Emma was a defector in more ways than one.

Your mother asked about the baby, calling it It. The landlady said It wasn't all there, said she had been informed by the matron of the hospital, a thing Emma had not the breeding to do.

The telegram made sense at last and your mother was exasperated at not having divined it correctly. The landlady said bad blood, but in a callous tone, said she herself did not rule out foul play. She said that Emma was in league with medical students and veterinary students and that that spoke for itself. She said there was a certain volume called Gray's Anatomy and what it didn't contain about the human body in text and diagram was nobody's business. She said it was her contention that Emma had tampered with it, took things to hurry it on and wore a corset right up to the last day which was enough to deform any child.

Your mother was flabbergasted. Then she let fly. She said there was a set of sins called backbiting, calumny, and detraction but that that insinuation topped the lot. She was shaking.

The landlady said never was there smoke without a fire. Your mother said what nerve and then the landlady got ferocious and spouted the contents of your mother's letters to Emma over the months, in which there were degrading things about the landlady herself and constant barging about money. The landlady said it was no wonder Emma was a hussy seeing the homestead she sprang from, seeing the lack of breeding.

Your mother praised her own acres, boasted about the thoroughbred horses. The landlady told her to keep her voice down. Your mother said to you that you must leave immediately and not consort with such folks. Folks sounded very out of place. The landlady said there was no point in going to Father Scanlon either because he had washed his hands of her. Hardly had you stepped off the mat than she closed the door on you and grazed the backs of your heels with the big draught-excluder.

In the hospital there was a funny smell. She said that smell brought back memories. It was ether. A clouded smell.

At first you could not find anyone to direct you. You could hear babies crying. The almoner told you the date when Emma had checked out. Emma had not sent the telegram until she was ready to be discharged. Emma had done a disappearing act. The almoner consulted a chart and read out her full name and the baby's name. It was a boy and weighed five pounds, twelve ounces. Emma had called it St. John Aubrey. There were no relatives of that name. It was in an oxygen tent. She said that in view of the situation there was no question of your being allowed to see it. She said it would be in the tent for weeks but that it was out of danger. Your mother asked about deformities. The almoner was furious, said there were no deformities but a blood defect. Emma's blood and the man's blood were incompatible.

A trolley was wheeled by but you didn't look. Your mother said afterwards it was lunches with aluminum lids over them. You were both starving. You went to a restaurant and had tea and buns and after the tea had revived her she went to use the telephone. The waitress who was elderly showed her how to put the pennies in.

She rang up Emma's place of work and was told that Emma had left five months previously and when she put the phone down she shook her head and sobbed and said she had lost a daughter.

You went to the three lots of lodgings where Emma had been. In one of the places she was not even remembered. Then began your quest. You realized the unpreparedness, the flurry of it all. She considered going to the police but shied from the thought. She went to the newspaper office and put an advertisement in the Personal column of an evening paper that she had a hunch Emma might read. She made the request to be reunited at six o'clock any evening, at the foot of the statue of the English general. They could not insert it for a day.

There was walking and waiting. She thought infantile things like that she might run Emma down in a shop, in the porch of a chapel or sitting on a bench in a park. You passed a place the Germans had bombed by mistake. There were weeds growing out of one wall and children playing on hillocks of rubbish. In every church you prayed for the same thing, to find her. You had no sense of direction and kept going astray. She searched for Emma's bike among a consignment of bikes that were inside the gates of a cigarette factory. Some had padlocks on them. They were all jumbled together and balanced in such a way that when she put her hands on one an assortment of them collapsed and the two of you ran in mortal terror. It was about the only moment of levity you had. Sometimes in one of the main streets she stopped and looked at the clothes in the windows. She stopped without meaning to and selected the garments that she most liked.

You got there well before six. People were pouring out of the shops and offices. She remarked on them, how callous they were. There were girls with hair and hair styles like Emma's. That grieved her, misled her for a moment, made her think she had sighted Emma, coming toward her. You could see her too, you ascribed a certain coat to her, the turquoise coat with the half belt. It was worse than if you couldn't picture her at all. The same commotion was always going on at six, the throngs, the bicycles, bells clanging and clashing, huge queues for buses, and hardy weather. It was a relief not to be going anywhere, to be simply stationed.

You could have climbed to the top for a copper each but she was against it both because of the extravagance and the possibility of vertigo. The women who had been selling from barrows folded them up and hauled them off. They took hold of the shafts and were horses to their own carts and you could tell by their gait that they were ready to drop. The ground was strewn with butts, and toffee papers and lollipop sticks, all from the day's diversion. A one-legged man played a mouth organ, and his friend, who had a facial affliction, coerced people for money. The one-legged man had his trousers pinned up so that there was no overlooking his condition. She fobbed him off with a miraculous medal, said it would improve his voice, give it timbre. She felt certain that it was on the third day Emma would come. She clung to that.

A window was decorated for Christmas, well in advance. All nightgowns had *Pleasant dreams* placards on them. They were long and gossamer like dance frocks. She thought Emma might be window-gazing.

The stars were not nearly so bright in the city, not nearly so singular. Between you and them there was a pall, a pall generated by soot and by smoke. Before the lights went out the sky had a coat of pink. She recalled her time in New York, the time of the green georgette and the dance shoes and multi-flavored ice creams. She said the Italians were great for concocting ice cream.

The smell of coffee from an ice-cream parlor was agonizing. It plagued you. So did the sight of little oranges wrapped in silver paper. They were packed in blond wooden boxes. The lid of one box was half open to display the contents. Dark tacks stuck out of the wood. You gazed and gazed and thought of William Wordsworth who had gazed at daffodils. Your mouth watered. She said only people with pull would be able to buy them and why have them in the window at all, tempting people. She was reminded of Manny Parker's sister and then remembered the amount of money she owed her which was catastrophic.

You missed home, you missed ordinary dull things like crushed stones in a field, and the wind, and the way it touched you on the face and its noises and the cattle too, an accompaniment to everything. The cattle in the city bawled, being cooped together in marts or waiting their turn at the abattoir. She inquired into the bedlam that started up at dawn.

Everything required money, the ice cream, the bus, the Zubes that she needed for her sore throat. In the public lavatory you slipped in together and once the attendant, who was a fiend, said it was not allowed. The same attendant recalled a woman to rinse the scummed washbasin after her. You were glad that it wasn't you. Passing cake-shops she recommended that you look away and sometimes you did and sometimes out of pure perversity you didn't, you couldn't.

She kept having a presentiment that she was going to encounter the man who was responsible for Emma's ruin. She vowed that she would cut him dead. You were keen for it. But each time passing the block of offices where he worked she nearly ran, although at all other times she hobbled.

In the evenings she had to pare her corns with a razor blade and allow her poor bunions to soak in warm water. The two evenings there was the same thing, stew. It was brown one evening and white the other. There was bread pudding afterwards but it was dry and unappetizing and without benefit of either raisins or spices. The hunger that assailed you out on the street left you once you sat down to eat.

You stayed in lodgings near a public park. Just inside the entrance there was a depot for training policemen and you watched them doing exercises each morning before breakfast. You imitated them. Your muscles creaked. Their navy-blue jackets hanging on the spears of the railing looked a bit like policemen too, only nimbler.

She asked for the tea in the bedroom so as to shun the other lodgers. It was insipid tea. The landlady used the old tea leaves again and again, put them to dry. They were drying indoors in a strainer. One lodger was an insurance clerk and the other a man who could not control his blinking. The insurance clerk tried to sell her a policy, kept emphasizing the benefits, the kudos he called them. She pretended to have a policy already. To get around her he told her some data about himself. He told her that on Sunday mornings he set his alarm clock so as to have the satisfaction of wakening up and being able to go back to sleep again. It did not work.

The other lodger was an amateur actor who kept repeating his lines out loud all through the supper. It was a very heated play about an extortionist boss and sweating workers and your mother said she wouldn't be surprised if he was a Red. The landlady, who was a widow, said she specialized in male guests because they were less demanding.

You would have liked to sit in her snug kitchen and confide in her but your mother said not to dare. Your mother pretended to be attending auctions on the quays, looking for rare pieces of silver. The landlady, for no reason, said she herself could have managed a chain of hotels if she wished.

Your mother said afterwards she was a boastful woman. She liked people to be self-effacing. You said the rosary together in bed. Often you said the three mysteries—the joyful, sorrowful, and glorious. Once after she had fallen asleep, you heard panting from the next room, the amateur actor's room. It was like something you had heard before, distantly, a footprint on your mind, you didn't know from where. He panted even though he was alone and it sent a kind of shiver through you and you prayed to God that you would never be alone in a city with no one to turn to at night.

After the third day when Emma had not appeared, she decided to go and see Father Scanlon anyhow. He received you in the hall of his house and he didn't suggest a cup of tea or any eats. You had never seen a priest dressed so informally before. He was without a jacket and it seemed to you he was like many another man or woman pottering around a house. His voice was censuring.

He said Emma had gone the wrong way, was well on the path of perdition. A libertine he called her. He said the terrible thing was that she had vocabulary and expression to ornament her various ideas and in that way she might exert power over others. He looked at you.

Your mother apologized for not being able to give him an offering for a Mass. He said Emma might consider herself the winner but that it was a Pyrrhic victory. He said she used the red herring common to all heathens, the one about free will. Your mother said if only they could find her. She went into a recital about the walks, the bicycles, the evening waits, and her nightmare in which Emma was in the gutter crying out for help, and not only prostrate but covered in sores, bedsores she reckoned.

Either he was moved to pity or he did not want loathsome detail urged upon him because immediately he touched the kid gloves, which she was clutching, and said he would do all in his power to find Emma. He was to be the hound of heaven. She thanked him extensively. He saw you both to the gate.

When you had gone a distance from the house your mother asked you what a Pyrrhic victory was and you had to confess that you did not know. She laughed. She suggested a pleasant surprise, that you have lunch out. You found a place but when you were installed she said she didn't feel at ease, had her suspicions about the kitchen. The two waiters were dark-skinned, and small. The moment you got their backs turned you left.

By evening Emma had been located. She was only a few streets away. Your mother kept saying it was a strange coincidence that you hadn't met going up and down to the center of the city, on a bus. Emma was out when you called but your mother had envisaged that and had already written a letter which she pushed through the letterbox. Then you both peered in at it. It looked very important, the one white envelope on the dark carpet. The place was spick and span and had an ecclesiastical smell. It enabled your mother to tell herself that Emma had turned over a new leaf.

Emma's reply was in a brown business envelope and marked personal. It was succinct. It said she was not bursting to see her mother, pointed out that she had just gone through hell with a neo-Victorian confinement and the loss of her child. Your mother said did anyone ever hear such impertinence, neo-Victorian and the loss of her child. While she was filling her pen she kept wording her letter saying she would tell Emma to come to heel, to come down off her high horse, to uncross the Rubicon. It was one of those pens that leaked if it was filled so she had to shake it to get rid of the excess ink and then almost immediately dip it again.

You were sent with it. Alone for the first time in the street, you were conscious of your appearance. Your coat was ridiculous compared with other people's coats. You took the scarf off your head and draped it over the back of the coat to obscure the big shoulder pads. It was a white scarf with the Eiffel tower painted in green on one corner and it was guaranteed washable. There was a drizzle. The tires of bicycles squelched on the wet road. You were terrified of knocking. The knocker was green. That was verdigris. Filigree was something else. You could hear footsteps inside. Eventually a girl who was wearing tattered slippers came out and said Emma had gone downtown. She told you the café where Emma had gone. There was nothing underhand about her. At the end of the hall a gleam of light showed through and there was a wireless on. You asked if you might wait. She said no. You assumed she had a boyfriend in there. She told you again how to get to the café.

When Emma saw you she waved like she was expecting

you. You smiled, you oversmiled. She was with two other girls. She introduced you as Little Sis and told you to take off the scarf, for Jerusalem's sake.

The thing that struck you most was her new poise. She had a navy suit on. It was very youthful. She patted her midriff and said she had got the figure back. That meant that the other girls knew about the baby so you congratulated her. She said Poor little mite and that was all. You said it was a good thing it was a boy because most people preferred sons. They all laughed. One of the girls said you were topping fun. It reminded her that when she was young she had a little dog and she tried to make him into a performer and took him in ripe cornfields to teach him leaps.

The place was lit with candles. Emma wore no blouse. The top of her slip was edged with lace in a contrasting shade of pink. It looked like something that had come from America. You had never known such atmosphere. The various candle lights were reflected in the window and so was their guttering which was fitful. The candles were in bottles that were crusted with grease.

The man next to you was eating squat red sausages. Emma said they were tomato sausages, introduced since the shortage of pork. The word pork prompted her into an impersonation of her boss. When in Paris at conferences he slapped his thighs to say lamb, for pork he snorted, and for tongue he stuck out his own tongue. He must have been in the meat business.

Emma ordered you coffee and a cream cake. You said grace so as to show her that you were loyal to your faith. There was an orchestra comprising a man and two women. They played a waltz. It was slow and alluring and you longed to say to Emma Will you dance, and you ached to be in her arms and she in yours and in that alliance to convey all the understanding and all the forgivingness that could not get said. You were daring yourself to ask her. She said to eat the cake with a fork. It was a bit messy. She was on a diet. You wondered if she was bleeding. Were her stitches out. Had she hollered in labor. What was labor. You wondered.

The violinist kept looking in her direction and it was obvious that he was performing for her. She told you to stop staring at him. Now and then she gave her head a little toss and the line of her hair moved in one straight line as if it were a cloth. It was very white, tow white like the sail of a ship. She said she was going to change her hair style, which was a Veronica Lake, because everyone had it now even factory girls. You said your mother was shattered. She said that was nothing new. The other girls were studying form, commenting on the boys and casting aspersions on the girls. The violinist lost his bearings, allowed his bow to go off course and made a ridiculous squiggle. The lady musicians took huff and one person in the audience booed.

When you laughed Emma tweaked your earlobe lightly and asked if you were clicking yet. You said you were not sure. The other girls conferred with each other, how you were not the least bit like Emma. You took it to mean that you were not so pretty. Emma said you had nice eyes, said it was the shape of an eye that counted, not the color, said people blathered on about brown eyes or blue eyes whereas in fact the color was a secondary consideration. She said yours were almond shaped. You had never seen almonds, except ground, and then they were a yellow heavyish powder.

You gave her the letter and without any qualm she held it

to the flame of the candle. It made a small but noticeable blaze. The violinist smiled. He may have told himself that it was a love letter she threw away on his behalf. He looked foreign. He had a nose like the Pope's nose on a chicken, it was flat, and the nostrils flared at the end.

Emma wrote with an eyebrow pencil on one of the white paper napkins and before folding it she held it up for you to see. It was a song that was all the go then.

> Now is the hour
> For me to say goodbye
> Soon I'll be sailing . . .
> Far . . . across . . . the . . .

She said you could sing it or intone it as you saw fit. You could not plead with her. You could not inveigle her. You asked instead if she had a nice flat and she said it was only a stopgap. She said she intended to move to the south side but, that, gone were the days when she had to put blotting paper inside her shoes or iron her clothes by putting them under the mattress. Her eyes, her cheekbones, the set of her mouth, everything about her was more defined. They might have been done with a chisel. She had a smile. She had a secret. It was sewn into her. When she laughed it was brittle.

You were afraid of her. You said you had better be off. She said to please yourself. She gave you some change and called after you to mind the wolves but she did not convey you to the door. Going up the passage you tripped and it was something you had foreseen but could not prevent. On the way out you bought a cake. It was the only cake in the display case.

In the street the lights were out. The couples allocated themselves in doorways and alleyways, the way they did each night. They gasped and groaned, their mouths chirruped and their arms so encircled each other that their persons were indeterminate. They were a blasphemy. You ran. It was more assertive running over concrete. It drew attention to you. You tried to run on your toes. Your mother was waiting at the window. She did not start speeching like you thought, she went dumb. All the invective had gone into the walking and the waiting. She was at a loss, like a simpleton.

You described the proceedings, Emma's girl friends, what they ate, what you ate and then at the very end Emma's reluctance to see her. You sweetened that. You said Emma had to recuperate. The note was in little shreds along with your bus ticket.

She asked some little particulars about Emma's appearance and Emma's apparel but on second thoughts begged not to be told. Slowly she began to gather the belongings and drop them into the suitcase. It was time to go. She had already secured a promise of a lift on a paper lorry. She had not done it personally but the driver was the dressmaker's nephew and she was supposed to have written and squared it. You waited outside the door of the newspaper office. At times you stood out from the wall in an attempt to half sit. It blackened your hands and blackened the seat of your coat but she did not scold you. At other times you walked up and down to get warm. The cold did not seem to affect her. She was thinking. What was she thinking?

Directly opposite was the river, the city's brown river whose waters were alleged to have a peculiar softness but had no salmon leaping in it. You hadn't tasted it direct. It wasn't like Lourdes or a place where waters were passed around for cures, it was not a sacred river.

She seemed mesmerized by it, kept staring, as if something important was going to emerge from it, a monster maybe. It had a tide like a sea tide. It lapped back and forth.

The moment the newspapers were ready a bustle started up and very young boys emerged through the revolving doors, shouting. You would not have recognized the name of the paper only that you already knew it, so garbled was their speech. It was jargon, it was sing-song. They scattered in different directions. From the back of the building the engines of lorries started up and she hurried around in search of the Samaritan who was to bring her home.

You stood holding your cake box. The loop of the twine was like a ring on your little finger. It had eaten a ridge in your flesh. A couple of drunk men going by tried to engage you in talk and called you stuck up because you wouldn't reply to them. They were very amused by the cake, the way you held it, they pretended to be carrying cake boxes themselves and tiptoed back and forth past you ridiculing your daintiness. You went toward one of the newsboys to be rescued. It meant buying a paper. It had a funny smell and the print was moist. Down at the end of the page there was a line that had slipped away completely, a sentence that had no end. You moved into the porch to read the headings.

CHEAPER CLOTHES COMING

REFUSAL TO REMOVE AXIS DIPLOMATS

DISCIPLINE PROBLEMS IN PARIS

The woman's nephew had had no warning but he gave you a lift all the same, even though it was against regulations. There were two other passengers, a man going home for his father's funeral and a man who had to till his fields because they were in danger of being confiscated. You all had to sit in the back so as not to be seen. You each sat on a bundle of newspapers. They served as cushions of a kind.

You were a somber party. The man going home for the funeral had a fawn teddy-bear coat which meant he was prosperous. You were tempted to stroke it. A teddy-bear coat was one of your favorite garments.

In each of the towns a bundle was dropped outside a news agent's door. The people were sleeping. The towns were the color of the creamery tank, pewter. You said their names, you knew them off by heart, that long litany of names that charted the journey from the city to where you were conceived and born: Leixlip, Mountmellick, Port Darlington, Toomevara, Cloughjordan, Borriseykeane, Kenigad, Nenagh, Portroe—towns and townlands, meadows and chieftains, raspberries on canes, sundials and hounds and hallways, and two-roomed houses with a tangle of roses and damp clay. To think of such things was balderdash. Your mother would say so. Miss Bugler would not. Miss Bugler was in love with a married man. You saw them. She did not duck down, made a point of moving her head ever so haughtily on the axis of her long white neck. She was in love with Guard Cody. They were in her car but he drove it. They were parked in a lane. He had a jacket on instead of his tunic. They appeared to be talking gravely but you knew that in the dark they would hearken to one another and hold each other, and kiss. That was love. Love was a condition of the heart, a malady. The heart was sachet-shaped. One day you would fall in love, one day, no, never.

He made a detour to drop you by your own gates and when he refused the offer of tea your mother insisted on taking his name and address so that she could send him some table fowl. He hooted as he drove off and the dogs, roused from sleep, came down to meet you. They came slowly, half-heartedly, they were not nearly so buoyant as when your father arrived back from the monastery.

She made no reference to the baby, she simply said the end of an epoch. It would never be mentioned again; it would never be referred to, by name. You would pray for it, you would include it in your morning and night prayers, its welfare, its blood, and the hope that someone would take pity on it in the orphanage and pamper it. The sky had puffs of pink that were moving about aimlessly. The house looked cheerful enough.

Your father sat up in bed. He cried when he laid eyes on you. The skin falling away in folds from his Adam's apple was like a turkey's, slack and reddish, made him appear an old man, be the grandfather that he both was and wasn't. He said he hadn't slept a wink or had hardly broken his fast and your mother said it wasn't all malarkey in the city either but she was not going to relay it.

He was thrilled with the paper. He thought it an ultra-modern thing to have a daily paper before the day began at all. The bedroom was cold. Your mother carried up a tray. The cake was yellow and she swore that powdered eggs had gone into it. A new patch of damp sprawled across the fireplace. It was overlaid on all the older patches that had disfigured the wallpaper and it was more drastic than any of them. He said there had been a deluge. They compared rainfall and it turned out that there had been less rain in the city. He said you ought all to move there and she said no, not for love nor money.

He was reluctant to ask about Emma, but at last did, said

Well how was she, and then could not bring himself to utter
her name. Your mother said she was her willful, capricious,
and wayward self. She said she would tell him later. She
winked, implying there were incidents she could not disclose
in front of you but you knew it was a ruse to break it to him
gradually and give him less of an excuse to go on a binge.
Under the unlit lamp there were bills. Paraffin oil had trick-
led down and stained them. She knew what they were without having to ask. There was one from the major for the
horse's keep and there were rates and one from a corn mer-
chant for seed corn got a long time before.

He looked at you and said he was financially embarrassed
and you thought that the most pitiful thing he had ever said
to you. He would sell another field. The estate would get
smaller, the boundaries close in. At last there would be your
own house only, your own house would become an ark, with
cats and dogs and livestock and your mother and father and
you, tossed together, for eternity.

She said there was one favor that she would ask for. It was
a telephone. He said by all means. He would have given her
anything. He was full of largesse. He said he could pull it,
being a peace commissioner, he said ordinary people had to
wait years for a telephone, but he was no ordinary person, oh
no boy. That sparked him and so did the paper and so did
the cake although it was made with powdered eggs.

You were shivering both because the room was cold and
because you hadn't slept. She told you to get into bed, to
miss school. It was nearly light and lying down in bed you
could see the tops of the black trees and the flecks of snow
on the nearby hills. You were tired, and on the verge of sleep
and you thought of yourself as jogging along in the back of

the van through a succession of empty sleeping towns that were the color of pewter. She brought you a stone hot-water bottle. She put it at the end of the bed and you stretched your legs to reach it.

She did not go to bed herself because she was anxious to get things in order, to get bread baked, to get the hen house cleaned out, to get windows cleaned, to get things presentable again. The stone bottle was too hot. You pushed it toward the rungs of the bed and every so often you stretched so that your feet had the benefit of it but when it suddenly got unbearable you took your feet away. You realized that in hell you would have no such choice and the fire would be all around you, the tongues of flame touching every part of you, every zone and the devils would be all around you stoking it and hell and the sleeping towns and the jog-jog and the tongues of flame battled in your mind as you descended into sleep.

Miss Bugler was dinning it into you. You tried to sing from high doh to low doh. You could not distinguish between one note and another. You were tone deaf. She hit the tuning fork and asked you to take the note but you could not understand what she was talking about. The sound of the fork cleaving the air was a metallic one and you could not reproduce it in your throat which was composed of muscle and tissue. It would have been easier to attempt a bird's note.

You were studying for a scholarship. You were cramming. You promised that you would get it. You studied going home along the road and girls passed remarks. They sat in cliques, playing forfeits, and some went in pairs across fields to kiss and do things.

You had kissed no girl since Jewel went away. She used to use some of her mother's lipstick that smelled like raspberries. You could summon up that smell any time you wanted, and taste it too, its fragrance.

The boys went home in cliques too. The boys were in a different school. Their teacher was descended from the Huguenots and had a flaming temper and got beset by more than one parent for doing grievous bodily harm.

Your books had marks, thumb marks, daubs, various pressed flowers, and bits of nose pick that had shriveled and dried. You ripped the oilcloth covering off old books and covered those new ones that were in danger of dismembering because of being put to so much strenuous use. There was a shortage of brown paper. The pressed flowers went putrid, the sweeter they'd been, the more putrid they became. The books were bound with yellow gauze. You preferred those that had big print and decorative capital letters. When you brought the print right up to the bridge of your nose, you lost sight of everything. That was called not being able to see the wood for the trees.

In the morning you tried to memorize what you had gone to sleep chanting. Often sleep canceled it. You dreamed of a rubber dog having fits and of carrying vegetable marrows that were sprouting limbs, between the ridges of a ploughed field. Miss Bugler allowed you to take the infants' class, to practice the method of teaching. You sat on the floor in a corner of the classroom. They all sat around you. You sat very ladylike. They didn't care how they sat. Their knickers showed. The gussets showed. They played with plasticine. The plasticine was old and dry, the oils had gone out of it. The different colors were mixed in together so that it was streaked, but basically it was brown. They made figures and pots. They gave them names. One was called Giant's house, Giant inside sleeping. It was a topnotch.

You did not want to be a teacher. You wanted to be a specialist in a white coat with your nails varnished. Miss Bugler gave you extra tuition. She smoked in front of you. You sucked mints together. You had the wrong vocal chords for French. She said Oui, oui, oui, oui, but you could not grasp it. She was nice about it, told you to lose your inhibition. Your mother put your supper down beside you. It was boiled egg. She said to eat or it would get cold. If there was a blood spot on the yolk it meant you would pass your exam. There wasn't. The yolk was runny, she put the top back on it and stood the egg cup in the pot of boiling water to harden it a bit.

A man with a slashed face kept looming up in your thoughts, someone you must have seen in the city. Emma sent sausages for Christmas. Wrote Perishable Goods on the outside. She parboiled them to keep them from going off.

Christmas morning there was a row. Went into a tantrum because he couldn't find the suspenders to keep his socks up. She said he'd done without them all the year round so why the sudden impetus to keep his socks up. While he was still threatening to maim her she left for Mass. Luckily the turkey was already in the oven, sizzling away. There was a white frost. The grass was like ostrich feathers, each blade a plume of white. Her shoes and your shoes rasped. There were a few stars left in the sky, a few who had omitted to go. The trees were very stark with their characteristics showing, their knots and their tumors and their branches and their twigs. Some had tapering twigs and some there were with twigs like prongs, out to afflict. The gates looked imposing because of the whiteness, looked like gates leading to a palace. The cows had been foddered and the sops of hay in their mouths hung in loose wisps like beards.

That had maddened him, having to get up early and exert himself. It was less slippery in the gutter than in the middle of the road. You clung to each other for support. She had no money for the collection. She said she would have to pretend that she forgot and by the following Sunday have it scraped together. She had arranged to sell two old hens that were past laying, to the proprietor of the hotel. They would be served there for supper one evening to the residents and the visiting commercial travelers. You said Happy Christmas over and over again. People said likewise to you. There were twelve days and twelve nights until little Christmas and it was doubtful that they could all be happy, that they could all be harmless.

On the altar there were white flowers. You had heard about them. They had been sent from the city by a benefactor. The sacristan had told it in confidence. They were sent in cellophane with pillows of white paper between the blooms to keep them from bruising one another. They were chrysanthemums. They were at either side of the tabernacle in units of six.

Everyone went to Holy Communion except your father and the tailor. They were the only two people to stay kneeling while the entire congregation went back and forth to the rails, bumping into each other because of the half light and their solemnity. Your father must have broke out, must have drank tea to assuage his temper. The tailor must have touched girls' diddies. The tailor's wife had a hat with a feather. It was very lifelike and comical. When she moved her head the feather moved and it was like seeing a bird sauntering on a hillside. She was two ahead of you in the queue for the rails.

After communion you had this funny feeling in the pit of your stomach, trickly, the same as when you used to tickle yourself, only you did nothing to bring it about. You no longer tickled yourself. You thought it might be due to hunger because of having to fast before going to Holy Communion, then again you thought it might be a touch of religious ecstasy. You knew that saints experienced such things and levitated. You were fearful about the commotion your levitation would cause. It did not occur. When you were back to normal you dwelt on a treat that you were going to have. There was trifle setting in the vestibule and you conspired to go in there with a tablespoon and scoop big mouthfuls, with bits of peach and jam and angelica in each dollop.

The priest said prayers for peace. All the men used the same hair oil, a creamy one. Some were lavish with it. It lay in lathers on their crowns, on their hair, or in the absence of hair, on their bald pates. The bald heads stood out. There were quite a number of them.

After lunch everyone felt drowsy because of having overindulged. The Nigger ate seventeen roast potatoes and your Aunt Hilda was the runner-up by eating six. The Nigger had to stretch himself before going out to do maneuvers. Your mother disinfected the chair when he had gone, sprinkled Jeyes fluid on it and with the floor cloth wiped the rungs. Men assembled in uniform. Some had shotguns. They split into two groups, the attacked and the attackers. Your mother wiped the steam off the window and looking out said she could foresee consequences, an arm or a limb getting shot off. But she was laughing. Your aunt said wasn't it amazing how not one uniform fitted properly, how

couldn't they have swapped them around and been less hick-
ish about it. Your father said God help the country. Some
of the men ducked down and were bombarded by other
men. There were sporadic shots and a variety of reverbera-
tions. Those who did not take coverage in time had to act
dead. They were prostrate on the frozen ground. The dogs
found it invigorating.

You went outside. The sky was gray and woolly. The sky
was flocculent. The dogs unearthed some hares and rabbits
and what should have been a military occasion turned into a
hunt. Your mother said with a bit of luck they might kill a
fox. There was a five shilling reward if a fox's tongue were
presented at the barracks. The sergeant used one as a mascot
in his car.

The following Sunday the priest referred to the maneuvers and said coordination was called for. A cousin of yours
came and made them do marching, do left-right, left-right.
Then a battle took place. One unit had to advance and be
ambushed by a smaller unit. The ambushers threw grenades,
which were clods of earth, at the marching troops. The men
that got clouted were livid and lost their tempers and it all
became very personal as those that had long-standing
grudges against each other took the opportunity to take re-
venge. There were fistfights with other echelons on the side-
line cheering and spurring things on. Your cousin said it was
a real fiasco. He took a clothes brush to his uniform. Your
mother admired it, the cut and the cloth. He said American
taste was best in everything. He was a G.I. He had a twang.
He had come from Germany to look for graves and ancestors
but your father was the only thing he located. Your father
asked him was he afraid in the trenches and he said not ex-

actly. They said unfathomable things. She called the white frost black and the Nigger said it was too cold to snow even though snow was the coldest thing there was. Your cousin exposed his chest to you. It was sinister. It was densely matted with black hair and he had nipples and they were mauve. They protruded.

He crooked his finger and said Come here, Honey, come, come to me, and you ran, went by banister for fear in your trepidation you might have capsized down the stairs. You ran out the front door and down the fields and past the fort and through the lily swamp to the callows. You saw the dark coming but that did not deter you. You kept running away, away from the house, where he was packing to leave. The light went under the trees. Under the trees began to be vast dimensionless places. It was the worst light, because of being creepy, because of being over-suggestive. The dark rose in spines around the trees and the bushes and the new telegraph pole and they were distinguishable as tall shapes in a thicket of deeper dark.

You prayed to your guardian angel. Your guardian angel was a tall dark man. So was the Devil. So was your cousin. It made you crawly to think of his chest. His chest was infested. A pediculous place. An occasion of sin. The branches acquired their nocturnal shapes. They were beasts of prey. It was the blackest time before the moon and the stars came to light the way. You arrived at the river.

The two swans were there, stately as ever, the same two who presided year after year. They never had any young. The river was in flood. You went through the labyrinth of reeds down to the water's edge. They were wetter than grass. They had harbored the rain. At the far side of the river and three fields away, there was a road on which the wheels of a cart rumbled. You shouted. You shouted with all your might. You shouted Help. You could hear your own voice, then your echo. You had no idea what would come to you, a kindly person, a ghost, or the Nigger who might nail you down and do pooly in you. He rampaged at night to look at celestial bodies.

There was no response save the rushing of the water and the bats and in the distance dogs and other carnivorous things that you could not name. It was a mistake to yell, a cardinal error, you only drew attention to your plight. You couldn't move. Your legs were going from under you. Your legs were liquid, were like snot. You couldn't retrace that long, terrible, vicious route again. You couldn't move. You had to. You ran through swamp, through high grass, through not so high grass and through the woods. Your speed was wizard. Nothing impeded you. You got wet. You got covered in mud. Your sweat was streaming. There were assemblies of briars, as high as you and higher and when you approached them you closed your eyes to intercept the thorns. It did not matter that thorns got in your flesh, anyhow it was unavoidable. When your dress caught on a briar you ran on without turning round to free it. It freed itself. The noise was like the tearing of a sheet or a bandage. When you saw the kitchen light you slowed down and when you got close to the house you leaned against the hedge to get your composure back.

She said your cousin had not left a shilling or a box of chocolates for you. She said that was chivalry for you. When she saw your injuries she exclaimed, asked what had happened to you. You said you had lost your way. She said to stop sounding like a little lady in a sonnet like Lucy Grey.

The cuts fizzed when she put peroxide in them. Before taking out the thorns she sterilized the needle, she let it suffer the flame of a candle.

You walked in your sleep. She said a step further and you might have walked out the window. She brought you to the doctor. She thought it was worms. He squeezed your cheeks and asked if you had seen a pooka man. You said no. He said to slip out of your clothes. You went behind the screen that was from China. Both the frame and the silken cloth had seen better days. He tapped your chest. He put his stethoscope to it. You said Aah. He put a flashlamp down your throat. He frowned. You liked the prospect of dying, of having spotted lungs, then galloping consumption, of being in heaven with God and the angels, away from everybody. You envisaged heaven as an open-air spot with plenty of roaming white clouds.

He sent you to the nearest city to have an X ray. You had to wait your turn. A nurse gave you tea and cake because of being his patient. The cake was iced with coconut and the flakes lodged in your teeth. They were stale. She referred to him by his first name. She said he always disliked the stage shows she liked and vice versa and that that was the only divergence between them. While she was doing the X ray you had to hold your breath. You were afraid that you might let her down but you didn't, you held your breath until she said to you that it was all right and to breathe normally again.

The result didn't come for three days during which time your mother gave you egg flips which you swallowed in a gulp. When you heard that you hadn't consumption you went upstairs and lay on your bed, in rage. The teacher sent for her, said it would be better if you didn't take the exam, said you were too highly strung. Your mother said they would not force you, they were not believers in force. So did he.

You got to hate boiled eggs. You also had an aversion to mashed potato. You became a thief. You stole a slab of chocolate and when closing the sideboard door let it creak to its utmost to confound her. You tore the silver paper in bits, then whirled each bit into a tiny ball and put them in the coal scuttle where there were old cigarette boxes and a goose wing and butts. You gorged. She discovered you.

She took you in her arms and said she did not begrudge you anything, not anything, if you would stop being so mistrustful. Her fingers smelled of his scalp. She had been rubbing his head. He liked his head rubbed, also his back. During the day he often asked for a rub, called it a pick-me-up.

You went to the chapel. It was quiet except for the flutter in the rafters. Birds lived there. The sanctuary lamp hung on a long low silver chain. The silver had a dull gleam to it and the flame smoldered steadily. It meant Jesus was present.

You went inside the rails. No woman was supposed to do that. The consecration bell was at the foot of the steps. It was an ordinary brass bell and you were disappointed. You tiptoed out.

You said the Stations. You lingered at each one, studied the faces and the poses and the expressions until you got to the Crucifixion and then you rushed it. It was too gory. It lent itself to too much awful speculation.

You had a vision. You were with Jesus on a mountain road and he wore a white robe and was performing miracles easily. You were his assistant, you were carrying his equipment.

The sacristan came in and ordered you out of there, said she was about to lock up. It was so you wouldn't clash with the young priest, who was home on holiday. She was without her glasses and had a clean smock on. She was struck on him. Everyone was struck on him. One woman had swooned. He wore no collar, had rented a car, and was a connoisseur of table wines. His sermons were stunning. People were riveted. They were all the rage the way once upon a time the Prince of Wales had been and Miss Amy Johnson for her valor. He was very partial to Mary Magdalene and went into rhapsodies about her hair and the ointment with which she anointed Jesus.

No particulars were known about that ointment. You yourself thought it might be pomade. Neighbors gathered in his house each night to listen to the gramophone and play cards. And people hung around outside playing pitch and toss to get the benefit of the gramophone too.

Your father was yearning to be part of the merriment. Your mother said oughtn't they invite him up first, have a spread for him. Your father said by all means. Your mother devised it, a meal consisting of cold ox tongue with fresh beetroot and potato salad.

But he arrived unexpectedly when the breakfast things were not cleared away. She said all her grand schemes were kiboshed, hinted about the banquet that was to be prepared. He said he was not one for ceremony. He had a lovely tan. He also had freckles. He looked at you, fixed you with his eyes which were gray. The freckles were in a haze across the bridge of his nose.

Your father abandoned his outdoor duties and came in protesting that his hand was not clean enough to be shaken. Calves stayed at the gate bawling for their rightful quota of milk and the dogs had no influence on them and failed to

quell them. Your mother put an embroidered cloth at one
end of the table and got clean cups down. Your father and
the priest discussed whose hay had yet to be saved and then
got on to the war and the whacking that the Germans were
getting. The priest said he was neutral, that it was a priest's
duty to be. He described the tropical island where he lived,
emphasized its scenic beauty, its flowers, and said its chief
crop was sugar cane. He said the coconut was the indigenous
tree, and waxed eloquent about its slender trunk and its big
palms. He looked at you. He said the loveliness of a tropical
night could not be overrated. He asked you if you knew the
latitude and longitude of his island, or why Red Indians were
called Red Indians.

Your father said you knew your stuff but when it came to
being asked you got flustered which was why you didn't take
the examination. The priest pretended not to register that.
He signed in your autograph book. He signed on the very
last page, as if the book had come to an end, which it hadn't.
He hawed on it before closing it. It was a secret:

> My body is but a cabbage
> The leaves I give to others
> But the heart I give
> To you.

You wished that Emma were there so that she could see.
You thought how you would love to go to the tropics with
him and see people who offered mangoes and sweet potatoes
to the Virgin Mary instead of flowers or candles.

He insisted on taking you all out. Your mother and you
ran upstairs to get into good dresses and put on Eau-de-
Cologne. You put a button-down dress on and left the two

bottom buttons open to be able to make greater strides.

You went to a hotel that overlooked a lake. There was a lemon tree and although it had no fruit it was a marvel to see. He was the one to point it out. You had cold salmon and then ice cream. You all had the same thing. He had a half bottle of white wine which he asked them to chill. Your father was not tempted. The label got damp and defaced in the chilling. He took you in a rowing boat. It was a joyride. You had only been on that lake attending funerals before.

At close quarters the water had different facets. Some patches were agitated, some lackadaisical and there was a whole sheet that was not doing anything at all, not falling in with the rest of the water's rhythm. The lake was not a single thing but many-faced. That was on the surface. There was no telling what went on down through the level of the water, down to the very bed. No one knew that, not even the fishes. The fishes only knew their own realm.

You passed two houseboats with names on them. You commented on them. He took off his shoes and socks. His feet were tanned too. Between his toes was still white and you were able to see how deeply he had tanned. He had been away for five years. Five summers had gone into changing the color of his skin.

The hills were very near, were like old acquaintances. Your mother said that there was no country so beautiful and how people never appreciated what they had. He said travel broadened the mind.

The clouds were sweeping the heavens. The clouds were the brooms, the heavens the causeway. Something went through you, a shiver. It had come out of nowhere. It was like mercury in a thermometer suddenly shooting up.

He gave you half smiles that only you could detect. Your father trailed a line and each time when it got caught in the engine your mother flapped. The trees from one island to the next seemed to be bowing to each other. Nothing was downcast, not the islands, nor the reeds, nor the trees, nor the chatting that went on. Your father said Blast when a bottle got itself tagged to the end of his line. At first they thought it was a trout and there was great excitement but when he found it was a bottle he reproached himself for not knowing better. He got indignant.

There were swarms of midges. Your mother said it was later on you'd feel the bites when you got under the covers and the heat aggravated them. When the Angelus bell rang the priest gave it out and you all replied very stiffly and it was like a service. Your mother reminded your father that they had to be back to milk. The cows suffered, their udders were pierced with pain if they were left unmilked too long.

Since Ambie's departure your mother milked but your father rounded them up. That was their pact. When your father was away drunk and then recuperating your mother went down the fields with a pail and milked them wherever they happened to be.

The priest said he was taking you to Hilda's. He didn't ask their permission, he simply presented them with a fait accompli. You got out of the back of the car and into the front. You couldn't think of anything to say. You sang dumb. He said that when he was young he used to think of a dream and then get into bed beside his brother and dream it. He said they were dreams about being a captain and a prince and a stowaway and a robber.

Hilda's gardener was mowing the grass. Sometimes he

stooped to remove bits of gravel and other nuisances from the lawn proper. It was on a slope. The mower ran away with him each time when he got near the bottom. He tipped his hat to the priest and said she was lying down. The priest asked how old were the monkey puzzle trees. The gardener made a guess. He made various guesses, all different, all inconsistent. The upstairs casement window was thrown open and Hilda leaned out.

She was bucking. She asked was he always so punctual. In her drawing room there was a trolley laid for tea. She was wearing a long dress and necklaces. There were pies with caster sugar sprinkled on them and white scones, quadrant-shaped. She passed things to him and then pushed the plate in your direction for you to help yourself. She said she never ate tea. She put her hand to her forehead and seemed to be burping discreetly to herself. He knocked on her wrist. He said Knock, knock, knock. He was very debonair. He said I'm ribbing you.

You wished that you were invisible. You wished that you were a gnat. They were having a lovers' quarrel. You sucked your cheeks. If you sucked for long enough you would have an oval face and not a round one.

He told her that she was like an oil painting, of the Renaissance School. Her dress was flame pink. All of a sudden she ran out of the room and she had to bunch it up in her hands, because being long it endangered her. He ran after her and called her by her name which he abbreviated. He called her Hil.

You examined the cups. They were bone china and English. They were more faded round the rims where mouths had impinged over the years. You studied the tea leaves.

There were storms in all three teacups. You stood up and smelled some flowers that were in a bowl. Their stems had been cut away. They had no nourishment except from the water that they were laid into. They were specially for the occasion. They were tea roses, the same but different. They had the same smell but different characteristics. When you looked into them without blinking it was like getting drawn into them, it was like a spell, getting drawn into folds and folds of red. They were different near the base, had different shadings, different gradations of color and all had unique centers. Some were worried-looking like a person and some agog. There were insects crawling quietly, making quiet, eventful journeys from one petal to the next, from one flower to another. There were no gaps in between. Insects did not have to use any ingenuity to get about.

You pitied them being packed so close together. You separated the fallen petals to try and do a design. It was a straight line. It was unadventurous. He came and squeezed your arm and asked what mischief you were up to. He said how soft it was. It was nearly fleshless but the bones were weak from the way he clasped it. He said that was why a cat played with a mouse, to make her soft, to loosen the muscles.

He brought you for a conducted tour of the houseboat. He knew where the key was. He had carte blanche to go there any time. When you stepped from the pier to the boat you knew you were taking a monumental step. He stood spraddle-legged in order to take your hand and help you over. Inside the cabin everything was on a smaller scale and you had to get used to crouching.

He started a conversation with himself the moment he switched on the engine. He was conciliatory to it, said Whoa and Easy and There. He steered with his feet. He did that so that he was able to stand up and look through a hatch and gauge where he was going. The village began to recede.

He made his way between the other boats and the buoys and the boulders. As soon as he was out of difficulties he turned to congratulate you as if you had been responsible. You stood on the seat directly opposite to his. A skylark went back and forth on a different jaunt from all the other birds and he moved his finger imitating its buoyancy and its swoops. He said that in the tropics the birds were bright and had bright plumage but that their songs were raucous. He liked dun birds with quiet notes.

He let the boat take its own course, let it drift. He sat on the edge of your seat, touched your knees a few times, then he unlaced your shoes, removed them, then your ankle socks. He said hadn't you better come down from your perch.

You ignored that. But not for long. You went delirious when he touched your toes and seeing how you reacted he was spurred on to take even greater liberties. You begged for mercy. You made all sorts of rash promises, how you would be good, how you would be bad, how you would never eat jelly, how you would dance a hornpipe, how you would do anything he asked. You had to crouch and he petted you across your lap and said what a nice friendly lap it was.

Consternation had brought color to your cheeks. Inside there was only the bed to sit on. You had to sidestep because of the narrow space between the bed and the table which was stationary. He found some spirits. It was the dregs from two bottles and not worth pouring into a glass. He gave you a choice. You wanted neither. He got the very last drop by putting his tongue inside the bottle. The tip of his tongue was very pointed. His arm came around you and sometimes it lolled and sometimes it was on your throat, tapping it. You wondered if he played the chapel organ. You could see yourself in the buckle of his belt, distorted and gulping, but nevertheless you.

When he went outside to throw the anchor the boat made a scraping sound as he hauled it onto a tiny incline of beach. You looked through the porthole and saw an expanse of stones that were startlingly white. There was something unreal about them as if they had just been showered from heaven. He said he hoped there were no submarines around. He began to undo your buttons. They slipped open. The buttonholes were for a bigger type of button altogether. He spread the dress at either side as your mother might. He lay on you but supported his weight on his elbow. He began jogging up and down. It was like being on a cart at night, being party to nice slow movements and with your eyes closed at that. You were not afraid. It was an honor. You thought of him in his gold vestments and him in his cassock going through the village concealed from the raving of the swooning woman.

He was more serious than when with your mother and father. You brought out the seriousness in him, that was your drawback. He said it was a moment snatched from all the other moments. He felt your flesh, pressed parts of it, like a doctor who was looking for different responses in you. Your movements got very coordinated. You moved together. You were like people dancing only that you were lying for it, supine. He said he could go through you like butter. He put his finger under the leg of your knickers and sought you out and said what kind and what cushy you were and you were moving up and down as if on a seesaw and his finger was not an enemy, not then.

When he opened his belt and you heard it clang on the table, you strained to sit up and you tried to impede him from opening his buttons because it was nakedness that you feared above all. And you gripped his wrist and he gripped yours and each other's wrists were locked and he was saying no and you were saying no but you were at cross-purposes. Never had the corneas of eyes bulged so. He opened his buttons, wrenched them open and presented himself and said to touch it. It was grotesque. The flesh all around it painted and raw. He said to touch it. You touched it on the snout. Your touch was fearful. You begged him to stop. You expelled his finger. He tried to part your knees, to prise them open, said it would be lonely for him, it would be unfriendly but you were petrified and you would not yield.

He caught hold of himself and preened and elongated it and squashed it and treated it like it was dough. Never were you more incongruous, never were you more unnecessary. He caught hold of your knee and ground his face in it and swung out of himself and swore to his Maker that he was doing a heinous and a hideous thing and he strained and he writhed and he imprecated, and begged for it to be over, for his joy and his agony to end. While he yelled a great gout of stuff shot out and there was a ridiculously short span between the first cry that was pleasure and the last that was one of shame.

It looked like hair oil, all over you both, but it did not have a cosmetic smell. The smell got in the back of your throat as if you had drank it which you hadn't. He did not look at you, he lay doubled over and said that God forgave everything and washed everything and made everyone spotless again. It sounded like a snowfall, snow over the land and a mantle over the shoulders of the people.

You cried. He cried. But separate. He wiped your legs with his handkerchief.

He stood up and retrieved his trousers and tied his belt snappily. He did his hair both with the flat of his hand and a small black comb. You wanted to stay longer, undo the harm.

You said you would write to him. He flinched but without knowing it. You could not have said a worse thing. It was clinging. It was like the sweet flowers between the pages of a book, destined to become putrid. He stood in the water and towed the boat out to where the level was deep enough. The blood rushed to his cheeks.

You offered to help but he declined that. A tuft of his hair and the smoke from his cigarette ribboned in one direction. A wind had risen. You would have liked a storm.

You tapped lightly on the open door so as not to give her a fright. Your father's boots were missing and you were glad that he was not there to cross-examine you. You had a lot of bluffing prepared. She was drawing a chicken. She went on with her task. The kitchen was flooded with sunshine. She had already plucked it and the wet feathers were in a pile on the table. You could tell that something was wrong by the tone of her Good evening. It was astringent. She took out the heart, the gizzard, the miserable little liver and the two uneven sized kidneys. Those bits that were useless she put on the same pile as the feathers but the giblets she put in a saucepan for making soup.

She said And did you have a nice time. You said Lovely. She said so you had made your debut. You curtsied, you laughed. She said how dare you be so brazen about it. You said what.

She looked at you and said What indeed. She said it was the most unkindest cut of all. She was like someone on the brink of a seizure. She was purple.

You backed away from her in case she should smell you, or smell him through your body. You put your thighs together, folded them like hands. They smacked.

She said to account for yourself from the time when they so fondly left you. You went into a dissertation about the monkey puzzle trees, Hilda's headache, the flavor of the scones and the way he dictated his own dreams. You embellished it. She said that was a grave falsification of the truth. You began to gabble. You contradicted yourself. You were a goner.

She said to continue. You said there was nothing you had left out. She said it was easily known that the hire car and the two-tone shoes were indicative. The craw that she had been pulling at burst. The brown tobacco-like content spilled all over the inside wall of the chicken. That was fatal, impaired the flavor, forever.

She ran to the tap to rinse it, then abandoned it and left the tap running and shot back so that she could proceed. She said you went to a certain house for tea and behaved like lovers. She said it had been disclosed to her that your eyes met more than once.

So Hilda was the informer. Hilda had telephoned them. And hell hath no music like a woman playing second fiddle.

You didn't know but that she had had you traced. You de-

nied that anything untoward happened. She said with what
alacrity you defended yourself.

When your father came in she threw you into the arena.
She said how you had turned on her like a tinker. First he
started to shake you, then he began to clout you. You ran behind her, begged of her to shield you but she said you had
made your adulterous bed and you could lie on it now.

He took the ruler from your satchel and gave you a few
preliminary strokes. You ran into the hall and he followed,
his boot in the divide of your bottom. You ran up the stairs
to the first room. Your intention was to get in there and close
the door and stay there indefinitely, the way people did in
walled cities during a siege. He flung it open and ordering
you onto the iron bed, he raised your clothes so that they
were bunched over the top half of your body, nearly engulf-
ing you. He dragged your knickers down and you thought
that then for certain he would see it, the smear. You sealed
your legs and tightened your body and you were as tight and
as taut as a bowstring. Because of that the blows reached
home.

He kept murmuring to himself, saying what he wouldn't
do to you would not be worth doing. The slaps resounded all
over the house. Each slap was followed by her plea from the
landing that that was enough. She did not come to behold.

You closed your eyes so that less could penetrate. You
counted, to give yourself occupation. You timed them. There
were more pauses than strokes. It may have been that he
changed the ruler from one hand to the other or had to keep
pushing his sleeve up. Each onslaught was a surprise because
he got more impassioned as he went on. The flap between
your legs began to heise up and down and you encouraged

that and the pleasure that you forsook when you expelled the priest's finger began again, and the tumult that should have been his to witness took place unbeknownst to him on that rattly bed while other parts of you smarted and cried.

It was after he had gone that your body began to make its grievances known. There were two different hurts, the one on the very surface of your skin like a scald and the other in the very interior where your marrow and your predilections lay. Parts of you shook for no reason at all. You had the rigors. With your eyes closed you saw the approach of dark. The dark got in in the juncture between your lids.

The room was not wholly quiet, the bits of furniture, the wooden curtain rings and the curtains themselves all stirred, maybe conferring with each other. There was tea being made. They were talking amicably. They were collaborators.

You set about calming yourself as if you were an outsider who had witnessed what had happened. The pains you visualized as black and blue, shapes you gave them, and little tunes. You got the pillow out. The bedspread was clammy but the pillow was cold. You pressed your forehead on it. You kissed it. It was edged with lace. It smelled of starch. You were not afraid to be alone in that room. That was how you knew something had changed. You prayed to God the Father, the Son, and the Holy Ghost.

You pictured them going to his house, battering on the door, his being defrocked, his being banished to a monastery for all time, his Holy Orders taken away. You sent messages to him to disappear. You sent them in the form of a prayer. You addressed him in the vocative case. You said Oh Father Declan, go this night before they waylay you. You thought of different ways of reaching him, all dramatic, all foolish, all involving the use of the supernatural which you did not have. You begged your guardian angel to tip off his guardian angel. The moment their conversation stopped you listened in case it was crucial, in case it meant the execution of plans.

On your back and bottom the lumps began to rise. Some were nodules and some had silken skins where they had already decided to be blisters. When she brought you refreshments she brought you no candle. She opened the door slowly to announce herself. She let it creak. She left the cup and plate on the floor beside the bed. There was no bedside table. It was an unused room, a boxroom. You made no gesture to thank her.

That night they journeyed back and forth and hither and thither, to the lavatory, both for natural causes, and to examine the cistern, to make sure that the ballcock was in its rightful place and that valuable water was not leaking away; they conferred with each other about closing windows and closing the hall door although normally on summer nights it was left open to ventilate the place.

You held fast. You did not rise to any of that bait. Even when she undressed you you pretended to be asleep and made the sounds of unwillingness that a sleeper would have made.

She put vaseline on you. You could sense her dismay by the way she gasped when she trained the candle. Your body, like your brain, was crammed with incidents. It had to its credit a seduction and a flaying in one day.

It had no proven memory of when it was born, it had only hearsay of that, her enema beforehand, the scabrous shaving, the semi-raw goose and the way they sang Red River Valley. It had all the years of fondlings, and strokings from him, from her, and cramps after you took senna, your first sanitary towel, the way she engirdled you each night, the saddles of bicycles, and capsizements on icy roads on winter mornings. You had never used a loofah but it was something you had an ambition to do. She kissed you on your back.

One of the girls who was down in the closets ran back and said she saw the priest go away. The closets had half doors like stable doors and gave the sitter a capital view of the world. She said his mother and father were with him and that his luggage was strapped on, on top of the car. That was how it was clear that he was gone for good.

There was general dismay, even the teacher was upset because he was supposed to have adjudicated a concert. Jewel's sister bragged about how he had visited them, how he had taken flash photographs, in their sitting room.

You held your tongue. You were like Emma, with a secret sewn into you. You were not going to dwell on it, not even to yourself, you were not going to reinvoke it, go back and forth over it, picking out the pleasure bits, the peaks. It was a bud that got nipped in the bud for sure. You were both like characters at opposite sides of the Hellespont.

They made no comment about his going away but you knew they knew because your mother said that the ladies might stop pluming themselves and be clad for Mass fittingly. Your father asked you to convey him over the fields. He bought special Pentecost water to sprinkle on a yearling. Her skin was like suede, like a doe's and she was roan in color, a roan spectacle who was cutting milk teeth. Her lineage was in a studbook and he worshipped her. He admitted that he was hot-tempered but said he meant no harm, that it was for your benefit and was to instill into you good conduct. He said one prodigal in any family was enough. Maybe you had wanted to vie with Emma in iniquity.

The marks made different headway. Some began to vanish. You put puce pencil around them to chart where they had been. At school they thought it was eczema because that's what you told them. It was known that it ran in your family. Scabs fell off.

The thing you had to be was fervent and more fervent and most fervent. You gargled with salt and water. You used lukewarm water because it tasted vile. You endeavored to be sick then. You couldn't put your finger down your throat but you could put a goose quill down there, and you did, and after you had been sick you covered it with leaves. It took time for your stomach to settle before you could eat a piece of cake and begin the penance again. You meant to put wire in your throat, the way she poked wire down young chickens when things got in their windpipe but you failed to achieve that. Another terrible flavor was sulphur and you ate it dry and it got behind your nose and throat and nearly suffocated you. But the moment you heard from Lizzie that it was good for the complexion you gave it up because that was a vanity and so was putting curlers in your hair or papers, to make ringlets. Lizzie was friendlier to you, gave you a piece of advice, said never to eat mackerel because mackerel were a very dirty fish and ate mice. She said to you that she had knitted a few matinee coats in case the baby needed them. You said it didn't. You told her it was taken care of. She said Sssh . . . and put her fingers to her lips though there was no one listening.

Later they invited you to sit by them, to sit, in the gloaming, to see the long dull day out. You never refused, you just never sat with them. That was your resistance.

You raged against captivity. You declaimed Robert Emmet's epitaph. You stamped and recited verses in a paddock. You scanned lines, then you separated the dactyls, the diphthongs, the similes, the puns. You put them in little compartments, were as methodical about it as if you were a cashier in a bank sorting money.

You consulted creatures as to what you should do, asked frogs their opinion. Frogs had learned the knack of being stealthy. Frogs had very good camouflage, were the color of surroundings, a greeny brown. You skipped, enumerating all the possible professions, although at heart you wanted to be a domestic economy instructress. You no longer skipped to see if you would marry a man called John. You grew an inch. There were ridges on your summer dresses where she had to let them down. Ridges that did not wash out and could not be totally ironed out. She had an idea about getting a knitting machine so that you could knit socks for people but immediately she abandoned that because none of you had business acumen.

Emma wrote and said there was no scope for you in the city, suggested a correspondence course. He was optimistic. He said something would turn up. The creamery manager said you could go there and train to be a buttermaker but your mother said that was too agricultural and that you were not strapping enough.

You were sent to the Nigger's with some dinner. Your mother took pity on him because he had lumbago for weeks and couldn't stir. She covered the plate with one that was exactly the comrade of it, to ensure that the food kept hot. When you got there he was up and frying something on the primus stove. He was talking. He was coaxing someone, a girl. He was coaxing her to eat. First he whispered. Then his voice gathered momentum. He said, Come on now girl, eat up, good for you, peg away me girl, sample the gravy, two fat sausages frying upon the pan, one for Michael Flannery and the other for Briget Ann, Briget Ann you're so excited you'll soon eat up the plate, Ah bad luck to me, Ah said Michael, there isn't half enough to ate. You thought how you'd tell at home that he had a girl, called Briget Ann and you peeped through the window before knocking, to get a glimpse at her. There was no one there at all only the Nigger himself and his belongings and the tossed bed. You couldn't fathom it. So you just dumped the dinner and ran off. Your mother scolded you because you didn't wait for the matching plates, said that would be the last she'd see of them. Michael Flannery was the Nigger's real name and he must have written that poem for himself. You mused over it.

You made yourself at home on the branch of a tree. That was your broomstick. You kept one of her best cushions here. It got matted from the rain. You went flying it. The dogs presided at your feet which meant the cows couldn't. The dogs took the opportunity to lick themselves, to scrutinize themselves for ticks and fleas and stand on their hind legs and proposition each other.

There was an over-all smell but you could separate them out the way a prism separated light. There was a smell of bark, of green branches, of nettles, of dung, of fresh earth, and stinking earth, of fungi and the Elder flower that grew profusely and was one of the chief components for the homemade wine.

The fungi looked like fritters but were a poison. For what had nature made them, or for whom? You thought of Marie Antoinette and how she had to carry her own little phial of poison in case she was set upon by barbarians. Local people used Lysol.

There was a smell from under your arms. To bask in it you had to keep the top of your jumper pulled out. That was a treachery. A taut neckline she had achieved with great pains by casting off stitches scrupulously. You tugged at it with both hands.

The flutter of the leaves brought on your trance. Hundreds of thousands of sycamore leaves all obeying the same wind, their wide green palms opening then tightening, letting in and keeping out the light, changing the prospect from indoor to outdoor to indoor, forever altering. It was the most lonesome hour just before dusk with all the colors going, all the streamers, the pinks and reds, and violets and indigos and blues, the lovely laneways of vanquishing light. It was weepy time. You said Hip Hip Hooray. That was your giveaway.

She called to know if you had seen the gray hen. A particular hen courted disaster night after night, by refusing to go to the hen house. She was a distinctive shade of gray, a nearly nonexistent gray, an erratic layer, a misfit. In the hen house when she shone the flashlamp hens began to fluster and jog their necks and move around stupidly on their narrow perches. They may have thought that it was morning or that Ambie had come back to kill them. Even the cock did not acquit himself, did not do anything about defense. It was easier to count them than search out the rebellious hen because although her feathers were unique, the light was faulty and all hens presented themselves as shapes rather than as colors.

It proved to be nearly impossible because they started

moving about, getting down and roaming all over the dunged floor. You both arrived at different figures. You counted again, slowly, and arrived at the same one which was twenty-seven. It should have been twenty-eight.

She was both spiteful and commiserating. She went into a rhapsody about the morning, about the trail of feathers, of nearly non-existent gray. Those would be the breast feathers shed in fear while the hen was still being carried off. Nevertheless she ordered one last search. She rattled the lid of a bucket and prowled around calling Chuck chuck chuck and telling you where to train the flashlamp.

The hen's appearance was nonchalant. It was as if she didn't realize her error, didn't distinguish between day and night. Her pituitary glands may have been dotty. Your mother failed to catch her, or rather failed to hold on to her. For a moment she had her by the tail and then lost her. In trying to hustle her back in, three others got out and there developed havoc and consternation, with you running around after them and she in the vicinity of the doorway to make sure the whole batch did not come out. They kept doubling back on you and twice you were running in a wrong direction, because your brain took time to record where they went. You cornered two and with your hands, legs and outspread skirt you kept them there until she came to pick them up, because picking them up was beyond you, their agitations always made you drop them again. The third got herself captive by standing on an enamel basin that tipped up. Your mother literally flung her into the hen house and walking back to the house you were both short of breath. It was good exercise. You held the gate and lifted the strands of hedge so that her hair and shoulders did not get raindrops.

You were not lacking in friendliness but it was not the same, there was a breach for evermore. From the top step from which he ritually peed you turned around to say good-night to the night and felt a tear, tears for all the things that were beyond you.

The classroom got spruced up. There were ferns and branches in the firegrate and a smell of paraffin in the air. The windows had been cleaned with it and dunces asked to adorn themselves had douched their hair with it, for lice. The one girl that was a Protestant got sent home.

A nun was addressing the classroom. She said she had come for volunteers and because of the war everyone laughed. She passed a few remarks about how happy and how contented everyone looked and then she launched forth.

She said that when the Disciples followed Jesus and saw where he lived they stayed with him all the rest of the day. She said that was only figuratively speaking and that they stayed with him all the rest of their lives, apart from Judas who betrayed him with a kiss. She was asking for followers for Jesus. She said to open hearts and minds, to consider the vast domain of his need. She mentioned places, Bethlehem,

China, Burma, Korea, the Philippines, Africa, the pagan Orient. Distant places with drums and rattlesnakes. She said to think of the souls that needed saving, the children that needed baptism, the dying that needed extreme unction before being consigned forever to the cauldron of hell's fire. She said bonfires on the hills in summer were as nothing compared with that world of eternal flames, that Gehenna where the worm dieth not and the fire is not quenched. She emphasized that fact, how the heat had been going on for thousands of years, a heat that never slackened, was furbished by each newcomer, that dynasty of writhing and roaring with the Devil and all his assistants rejoicing over each soul's irredeemable loss.

You could have wept for the poor Protestant girl. You stroked your arms to soothe them, to remind yourself that they were still cool, that they were still on earth.

Those in the front row got sprayed with her spittle. The excess saliva hung in bubbles around the corners of her lips.

The younger nun kept her head lowered and had her hands submerged in big black sleeves. Her hands may have been her vanity the way your eyes were yours and her platinum hair was Emma's.

Mother Baptista said that the love of Christ was the only true sweetness, the only melody, the only goal. A mother's love, an earthly marriage, fame and fortune, these she said were as nosegays compared with the harvest of love that was Christ's. She said he was everywhere, in the room with us, in the playground, bent down with pity over some coolie dying of dysentery in the blistering heat, in the tabernacle, as artisan, good shepherd, savior and truest friend. Then she quoted the number of pagans in the world and everyone gasped, even the teacher who had become one with the pupils because of sitting with them at a desk, all attention, with her arms folded.

Mother Baptista said to cast one's mind over it, that figure, that outrage, that lamentable state of affairs. She said not to shrink from it, not to turn away from God's question, not to put it in the back of the mind like an awkward question but to look at it and to pray to God for guidance in answering it.

Out of habit you started to pray and she caught your eye and seemed pleased by what you were doing. She said they were not extortioners and that she realized you were all very young but to remember that there was nothing so dear in the sight of God as children and to remember the example of Jesus who said Suffer the little children to come unto me.

Some of the infants who had been sitting on a bench took it that she was talking to them and rose to go to her. That caused another bit of laughter.

She showed photos of the mother house, the house where girls went and trained. It was in Belgium. The photos were passed around and girls were frantic to look at them. It was an old rambling château with shutters and creeper along the walls, a haven garrisoned by angels. She said they grew nectarines and that in season they had them for breakfast. Girls licked their lips when they heard that.

Then she got very down to earth and asked what was a vocation. She posed the question three times before answering it. She said it was no angel appearing in blinding splendor, it was something deeper than that, more inherent, a desire to serve Jesus, to love Jesus, to be the spouse of Jesus. She said to think of the opportunity of being militant for Christ, of

being humble for Christ, of bringing pagans the happiness
he merited for them. She said we ought to make sure that
there was not one soul on earth for whom the blood of Jesus
had been shed in vain. She said in his time only male disciples were allowed to follow him but that too had changed
and women could take up the cudgel on his behalf. She said
yes, it was a marriage to God, she admitted that most girls
wished for a marriage to someone but in that union of God
and woman there was something no earthly ceremony could
compare with, there was constancy.

In a more matter-of-fact voice she listed the standard re-
quirements; intelligence, of sound health, and of good moral
character. She explained that if girls went they were educated
for free with a view to becoming novices. It was like a summer's day inside your head.

She got very declamatory, she said Who is for Jesus, who
is for Mary the darling of Heaven and then she quoted St.
Paul, Come over to Macedonia with me.

No sooner had she stopped than you raised your hand
and said you would go.

The girls in front of you turned around and let out different sounds but mainly ones of dismay. You were the focus of
attention.

She said there was no need to decide there and then as she
had not expected to be taken so literally. You said you had
decided a long time ago. The teacher nodded, said she had
thought as much, said you were a paragon and that tempo-
ral considerations were not yours. The others got sent out to
the playground.

The younger nun was twittery, asked what your name
was. She couldn't stop smiling. The elder nun said what did

your parents think. You said they didn't know as yet. She said parents had the crown of authority and how you must be guided by them in all matters. You nodded. You would go away from them, far, far away, where no conveyance could bring them to you.

Going through the town you were waylaid by people, shopkeepers who had always shunned and slighted you. It was as if you had already entered, so shy and respectful were they. It was like winning a trophy. You refused the various offers of tea and lemonade, the tactics so as to delay you, to stop you in your tracks. Girls tagged along to partake of your glory and asked if you would send them scapulars and medals and things.

No one knew anything about Belgium except that lace was made in Brussels and that in the field of Flanders there were poppies and soldiers. In your mind they were interconnected, the scarlet poppies and soldiers' blood. The dressmaker said you would have to hold yourself better as you were inclined to slouch. She never liked you, she had favored Emma.

The first thing your mother said was to give her a chair. She was alone in the kitchen pulling a sock together. The hole was too vast to be darned. She said what, what were you saying.

You told her again. She looked through the window at a rainbow the so-called prelude of joy and she said never would it summon up anything for her but sadness and dire news. Your father came in. She was off in a canter about Ellis Island and how she nearly got stranded there with all sorts of people speaking divers tongues. He said there was no connection between a religious vocation and Ellis Island. She said he hadn't heard the worst yet, that this particular convent was in Belgium, in the maelstrom of war and want.

You were trying to comfort her by stroking her hair lightly, by saying wheedling things. There was a lot of electricity in it and single ribs clung tenaciously to your fingers. You told him the education was free. He liked that. He said Good, good. He said to give it to him step by step, the proceedings. You said first you would have schooling, then noviceship, then take your final vows and go somewhere, anywhere, maybe to Africa.

That was the last straw. She said weren't there cannibals in Africa and you said, quoting the nun, that you would be fishing for Christ. He said it was very nicely put, estimably put. She said her heart was finally broken, in pulp, pulped. That was how she used to refer to the doctor who'd crashed, the one they kept the souvenirs of. Yet the moment she heard the nuns were coming to discuss things she was up off her chair and feeling the oven door to see if the temperature was hot enough for a sponge cake.

Mother Baptista said what a promising postulant she thought you would make. Neither of them ate. It was part of their regulations. Your mother instanced your will power by telling of a time when, still a child, you were given seed cake and you employed yourself to removing each seed separately and methodically. They did not know what to make of it and your father made some joke about your mother being distrait. He plied them with questions. He wanted to know where they lived and what sort of furniture they had in their parlors and if they got big endowments from people.

She mentioned some famous people who had been sheltering there, incognito, members of a Russian noble family whom you had never heard of. He told her about his sojourn in the potato pit. She hinted about the persecutions in China but didn't harp on them, just referred to her dear dead sisters. She had photos with captions written in ink under them:

AH THANK YOU SISTER

TREATING THE SICK

CHATTING WITH THE FAITHFUL

IN THE NAME OF THE FATHER

EXAMINING A SORE LEG

SISTER WITH MEDICAL KIT

The younger nun was confabbing with you, about your best subjects. She taught you the Act of Contrition in French and gave you a present of a little French missal that was exactly the size of a matchbox. It had a gilt clasp.

You were in love with her. The radiance that was hers would be yours. You kept thinking toward a distant moment with you on a priedieu and nuns all around you, singing, and your parents and Emma in the gallery crying. You wanted to go there and then.

This is to warn you. Read this carefully.

You received two anonymous letters. One said that a letter had been sent to inform the mistress of novices of the type of family you had come from, e.g. your father a drunkard and your sister Emma a harlot. The other begged you, implored you not to go, said you would rue it, you would not stick it out, you would come home in disgrace and go mad the way women did who came home from convents. They were in different inks and the handwriting was different and yet you felt it was from the same source and your mother felt so too and they were not shown to your father.

He had to sell the proceeds of a field of corn while it still stood. It was a question of guessing the yield, of taking a gamble on it. He and Manny Parker stood there deliberating. It was more gray than gold. That gray did not stand in its favor, meant an excess of rain had gone into it, meant a lot of husk at threshing time, meant trouble. Here and there a patch had lodged, formed a bed big enough for a beast or a couple to lie down in. That was something that would never happen to you.

For an absent-minded person Manny Parker showed a vein of shrewdness, felt the ears, walked back and forth with his head down emphasizing the fact that it wasn't a transaction he was pleased to take on, hinted at it being charity. A pig in a bag Manny Parker called it and quoted the price that he would pay. Your father said if that's what you say. He didn't haggle. He was beholden. He needed it.

They repaired to the far side of a tree so that the notes could be counted cautiously, out of the way of the wind. You counted also. There were all kinds of notes, crisp ones that could cut, tattered ones, stained ones, and even one that was held together with elastoplast. Notes from all and sundry, paid to Manny Parker's sister for commodities.

He handed them to you. She said he got diddled. It was for your fare and for your uniform. You got togged out. You had to get shoes, stockings, three gym frocks, three blouses, a raincoat, an overcoat, galoshes, a shawl, two navy berets, vests, combinations, nightgowns, and a white divided skirt for tennis. When you fitted on the dark clothes it added years to you. You could have been in mourning.

She turned and asked if you were sure what you were doing and you said Yes, yes, and repeated one of those aspirations that were supposed to keep doubt at bay.

You gave up sweet things. You set yourself tasks, penances. When you were moved to speak you held your tongue. Everything you did was the opposite to what you wanted to do. You stood around the butcher's, watching them chop, chop chop, until the ax got right down to the fat and he had to give a few last vital blows, watching the bluebottles, watching things you hated. You cooked sheeps' heads for the dogs. Their eyes gazed back at you as you put the lid on the saucepan. When you decided to go to a dance they thought that a streak of devilment had got into you but it was so that you would have to cavort with and be clutched by men who repelled you.

The young nun wrote. She used violet ink. Her letter was chatty. It was about the recreation they had on a Feast Day and the long walk they took. Your mother said it might not be as grim as she imagined. You ticked off the days in your head not on the wall calendar.

You tore up your autograph book. You wrenched the pages apart and then threw the tiny bits in the air, the pink and yellow and white and aquamarine fragments that were like specters of tropical birds, fluttering and falling. You parted with your trinkets. A yellow bone bracelet of yours on one of the tailor's twins looked particularly fetching as she twirled it around and around on Sundays during Mass.

People asked how long more you had, asked you every time they saw you. No one referred to it directly, it was just referred to as the place. Only its corridors could you envisage. You knew there were bound to be lots of them where you would slink quietly in your house shoes smiling at nuns and answerable to God.

Lizzie had goodbye in pink icing on a cake. Sacco came specially for the occasion, quoted Alfred, Lord Tennyson, treating the matter as if you were going to your deathbed, said,

> Sunset and evening star
> And one clear call for me
> And may there be no moaning at the bar
> When I put out to sea.

The Nigger had taken it upon himself to make you a little trunk and your mother whispered to you that it would be so profane you would have to have it blessed when you got there. It was new wood, the same kind as they made butter boxes with, and it smelled like that. Ever since the day you heard him talking to himself you were more lenient toward him and he seemed to sense it because he had a conversation with you about the equinox gales. Hilda, who had got over her tantrums, gave you a pair of linen sheets, big enough to fit a double bed. You got slippers, a propelling pencil, handkerchiefs, a crochet set, and a boot-polishing outfit from the dummies. To thank them you separated the brushes and then joined them together again and the hairs cleaved to one another as if they were magnetic.

You were dreading a speech. Lizzie boiled the kettle on the primus because it was quicker than the turf fire. The old people were hustled in the bedroom and Mr. Wattle kept asking pointedly when all the strangers were going to be on their way.

Your aunt talked of how it was only a short time ago that she had knitted dresses for you and bordered them with angora and she said how particular you used to be about those scalloped borders, decisive about the colors you wanted. Sacco said what a genius Churchill was turning out to be, a second Bismarck, a nab tactician. The doctor was to have come but the tailor's wife was having a baby and being over forty there were complications attached. Your father said it wasn't the Germans you had to fear now but the Reds and the Red Scourge. He said he had information firsthand from the nuns. He would have mentioned the priest also only that his name was taboo for all time.

Someone said it was up to the Pope to quieten those Reds and that the Pope had better do it, cathedra or ex cathedra, and the sooner the better. Someone else said that the Pope worked an average of sixteen hours a day and ate one meal and one small collation. Lizzie said that her kitchen was not the Vatican and to eat up. The buns had too much cream of tartar in them and scoured the back of your bottom teeth.

Hilda said she always regretted not having been a nun and

your aunt butted in and said she'd have wept to have had her auburn tresses cut off. That was a tactless thing to say because Lizzie had so little hair left she had to wear a skullcap indoors and out. Her hair was in a pile under a fine net, like a pin cushion or an ornament, on show. She had cancer. Everyone knew it but her.

From time to time Sacco raised whatever sweetmeat he happened to be eating and wished you bon voyage. He said life was a crucible. Your mother said life was a vale of tears. The Nigger said a fart. Sacco repeated the word crucible. Your aunt who admitted to not knowing what it meant was charmed by its name and said it again and again, crucible, crucible, crucible.

In your mind's eye you saw a small bone lid on which an object was being dropped from a tweezers and it turned out to be an eye that exactly fitted the circumference of the lid. A man's eye, a sheep's eye, any eye gray and without expression.

They discussed the vicissitudes of life. Your teacher was convivial with you. She said she would venture to say that you would persevere and take your vows and possibly carve a name for yourself in the ecclesiastical world. Your father said not to let the nuns boss you and not to forget your folks especially your illustrious father. The Nigger said that you were only a nipper and that there was no knowing how you might turn out, that you might become a Follies girl. No one agreed and no one disagreed. Only God knew that. There were no speeches.

The barley stooks were in huddles in the fields, the wind trapped within them. There were five stooks to every huddle, the heads bunched together, the hinds splayed out to achieve the balance. It was through these splayed ends that the winds entered and made a channel upwards. They were well done and none had fallen. They had been done by Manny Parker's men.

It created a certain spleen, seeing all those strange workmen with their strange dogs in your field for nearly a week of days, and having to boil kettles for them as well. You were saying goodbye to fields and to trees, and even to headlands of fields where a plow never got and where not an ear of barley had chanced to grow. In all these corners there were bits of things, machinery, broken delft, cowhorns that had served as funnels, machine oil tins and the rags and remnants that the scarecrows wore.

You felt a terrible burden as if something inanimate might

speak or something motionless might get up and move. You got over a conglomeration of briars and bushes that had served as a fence to the next field. The gate had fallen down. The fallen gate was like a grille inside the gap. Your new brogue shoes on the metal made a clang and when you saw the horses coming toward you, you climbed out immediately although you had dared yourself to go and make some sort of last rapprochement with them. It would be a year before you came again. Brussels was too far away for a Christmas and Easter vacation.

The blackberries were hard and wine-colored. You picked three and before eating them consulted them to see if they had maggots. It was all done out of habit, bits of grass picked, stems of grass sucked, stones touched to find the smooth spot, sudden runs, sudden halts, all senseless, all necessary. In the fort of dark trees you made a wish and felt a lily. You wished that they would be all right, that he would not injure her.

All of a sudden you decided that the car was probably waiting and you ran without having a last look at the chicken run or the tree that had been your abode for a period of time.

She was nowhere. She had left a cake wrapped in grease-proof paper and a pot of lemon curd that was still warm, having just been made. You were spending the night in a convent in the city and these were to be presented in the refectory toward your supper. You could have requested to see Emma but you didn't. The rift was complete. The following day you were making the boat journey to England and then to France, and then by train to Belgium. There was another girl who had also volunteered and you knew nothing about her except that her name was Bernadette.

Your mother's big present to you was a wallet with EDM written in gold. It stood for Enfant de Marie. You realized that she had been making it in secret over the weeks which was why when she went into the room she had insisted that nobody follow her.

He came to see if you wanted anything carried down. He was sniffing to dramatize his sorrow. He said to write if there was anything wrong, if you needed money, or couldn't pass your examinations. He said you had only to refer to the poem,

No mun,
No fun,
Your son

and he would send the spondulics by return.

To give yourself something to do you tried to close the window. Rain had come in. It was one of those windows that either closed with a thud or could not be budged at all. The glass had the dull gold smear of moths killed in June when she had run around the house with a rolled-up newspaper to batten on them before they laid their eggs. The stitches of pain under your ears were the worst you had ever had, were excruciating.

He helped you carry the trunk out. There were handles at either side. He said wasn't it inspired of the Nigger to consider the handles. Your name was in capital letters on the lid and you were ashamed of it, so boldly was it printed. In the convent a name awaited you, a saint's name, but you didn't know it yet.

He didn't utter a word to the driver. You ran back to see if there was anything you had forgotten. He followed. The handkerchief that he cried into was a scrap from the cretonne that she had used to make curtains with just before Emma's homecoming. He must have pocketed it then.

I will go now, was what you said, hoping that she would emerge from the house and say goodbye and have done with you, but since no such thing happened you went anyhow and the last thing you heard was a howl starting up, more ravenous than a dog's, more piercing than a person's, a howl that would go on for as long as her life did, and his, and yours.

Edna O'Brien's previous works of fiction include *Down by the River, House of Splendid Isolation, Time and Tide,* and *Lantern Slides,* which won the Los Angeles Times Book Prize for fiction. Her book about James Joyce was published in 1999 and excerpted in *The New Yorker.* An honorary member of the American Academy of Arts and Letters, O'Brien grew up in Ireland and now lives in London.

BOOKS BY EDNA O'BRIEN

Wild Decembers

"A page-turning narrative . . . as wildly beautiful and windswept as the country of her fiction." —*Elle*

Edna O'Brien's critically acclaimed novel *Wild Decembers* charts the quick but sure demise of relations between Joseph Brennan and Mick Bugler—"the warring sons of warring sons"—in the countryside of western Ireland, where "ancient feuds, romantic passions, and misguided ideas of fidelity blend together in . . . a heart breaking story" (*Wall Street Journal*). 0-618-12691-0

A Pagan Place

"A book whose genius is memory." —John Berger

In *A Pagan Place,* O'Brien returns to that uniquely wonderful, terrible, peculiar place she once called home and writes not only of a life there but of the Irish experience out of which that life arises. This is the Ireland of country villages and barley fields, of mischievous girls and Tans with guns. O'Brien recreates her homeland with singular grace and intensity. 0-618-12690-2

Night

"A brilliant and beautiful book." —John Updike

Edna O'Brien's classic novel *Night* journeys through one long sleepless night with Mary Hooligan as she recalls her fertile past, from her childhood in the Irish countryside to the love affairs she has confronted since leaving for English shores. This erotic reverie shows O'Brien to be one of the foremost heirs to modernism. 0-618-12689-9

CPSIA information can be obtained
at www.ICGtesting.com
Printed in the USA
LVOW11s1555160117

521117LV00002B/337/P